WOLFISH

Editor, journalist and mother of three cats, Kritika Kapoor is previously the author of *Batshit*. She lives and works in Pune.

WOLFISH

KRITIKA KAPOOR

PAN

First published 2024 by Pan
an imprint of Pan Macmillan Publishing India Private Limited
707 Kailash Building
26 K. G. Marg, New Delhi 110 001
www.panmacmillan.co.in

Pan Macmillan, The Smithson, 6 Briset Street, Farringdon,
London EC1M 5NR
Associated companies throughout the world
www.panmacmillan.com

ISBN 978-81-19300-62-4

This is a work of fiction. Names, characters, businesses, organizations, places, events, and incidents either are the product of the author's imagination or are used fictitiously. Any resemblance to actual persons, living or dead, events, or locales is entirely coincidental.

1 3 5 7 9 8 6 4 2

Typeset in Sabon LT Std. by SÜRYA, New Delhi
Printed and bound in India by Thomson Press India Ltd.

For Apoorva and Kashika, who have passed the test of true friendship by bravely suffering through my terrible first drafts

For Shwetank, the best thing to ever happen to me

Search for: Tara Tandon...

... Tara Tandon **author**

... Tara Tandon **books**

... Tara Tandon **Wild Nights with the Werewolf**

... Tara Tandon **Hot for the Hunk Next Door**

... Tara Tandon **Sexy Nawabs of Hasseypur**

... Tara Tandon **toxic?**

... Tara Tandon **misogynist?**

... Tara Tandon **cancelled**

haarsh
@Haarshcritic

I can't believe women still read and write such trash. Smh. It's the same plot every time, with the same dumb heroines and their unrealistic fantasies. Forget calling it literature, how is this stuff any different from pornography? @TaraT

1:11 AM · Mar 19, 2023 · Twitter for iPhone

8 Retweets **5** Quote Tweets **39** Likes

sappho
@Firstnamelastname

Narcissistic, controlling, borderline-abusive hero – check. Virginal, trembling heroines with no outward agency or self-esteem – check. @TaraT has abused the already much-abused bodice-ripper, much like the heroes in her novels love abusing their heroines.

10:42 AM · Mar 19, 2023 · Twitter for iPhone

2.4K Retweets **511** Quote Tweets **18.7K** Likes

Vik
@Vikas_567894100

First vampires now werewolves. Is this seriously what girls want???? No wonder i can't get a girlfriend. Females like @TaraT are the reason nice guys finish last

3:46 AM · Mar 19, 2023 · Twitter for Android

108 Retweets **21** Quote Tweets **2.6K** Likes

voices for equality @WokeTheTalk · Mar 19, 2023

The Problem with Tara Tandon Novels: A Thread

(TRIGGER WARNING - Sexual abuse)

276 12K 85.2K

voices for equality @WokeTheTalk · Mar 19, 2023

So far, I haven't commented on @TaraT's latest werewolf debacle –The Wolf's Captive (I mean, girl, really? How are we still doing Twilight in 2022?), because I have better things to concern myself with than her terrible writing and toxic cishet nonsense.

69 8K 76K

voices for equality @WokeTheTalk · Mar 19, 2023

But DAMN, the straights really don't seem to be okay. Watching her
half-assed apology on Instagram has really made my blood boil ... I mean isn't this woman like 30 years old or something?

68 1.3K 65.3K

voices for equality @WokeTheTalk · Mar 19, 2023 ···

Her argument – that her books are mere fantasy, and she expects the audience to be discerning – is as naive and dangerous as the toxicity she is peddling as 'romance'. The fact that such books exist & are so popular reveals the rot in heterosexual relationships today, and the work that still needs to be done in the post-MeToo world to dismantle it.

67 1.1K 63K

voices for equality @WokeTheTalk · Mar 19, 2023 ···

The truth is that @TaraT's werewolf – Waris – is an alpha-male asshole who makes Kabir Singh look like a saint. Even worse, his narcissism, misogyny and deep-rooted anger issues are painted as 'sexy' in the latest book. And while Waris is just as devoid of personality as Laila, at least he has one thing she doesn't ...

66 989 60.2K

voices for equality @WokeTheTalk · Mar 19, 2023 ···

... agency.

Because honestly, despite the endless red flags, why does Laila refuse to dump her abuser? Is it because of Waris' gaslighting, or the lack of self-worth gifted to her by the author? She doesn't seem to have an arc beyond 'fixing' this

emotionally stunted man-child (or wolf-cub?)

65 458 54.9K

voices for equality @WalkTheTalk · Mar 19, 2023 ···

+ don't even get me started on the sex, which would be funny if it weren't so triggering. Apart from the overuse of Victorian euphemisms (Her wet triangle? His manly protrusion? It's like sex and an alien invasion rolled into one!), the most appalling thing is that Waris and Laila only seem to get turned on by ONE thing – lack of consent. To them, humiliation, berating and stalking is the ultimate foreplay. Who hurt them? And in turn, who hurt their creator?

64 380 49.6K

voices for equality @WalkTheTalk · Mar 19, 2023 ···

I'm not saying that such books need to be banned, or that it's even POSSIBLE to ban them. But it just boils down to – is the cheap titillation these books offer worth the devastating blow they deliver on women's self-esteem? Is selling abuse as romance really justifiable under the guise of 'oh, it's just a fantasy'?

63 295 48.7K

1

It's over, and Tara knows this. She tries to explain why to Sameer over the phone, while standing outside a crowded Hauz Khas bar at 11 p.m.

Mindlessly sucking on a cigarette, she shoots a dirty look at the people staring at her – even though, right now, she is quite the spectacle with her shrill voice, bleeding mascara and short skirt. She's so drunk, she can't help swaying as Sameer continues to plead, 'So that's why you're gonna break up with me? Because I am a "nice guy"?'

She can imagine him using air quotes as he says it, because he always does, like it's 2001 or something. He calls himself a 'nice guy', as if he's doing her – or humanity in general – a favour.

Actually, that's exactly what he thinks he is doing.

He'll get this noble, pious, faraway, *I'd-like-to-thank-my-mother-father-and-dog-for-this-award* look in his eyes when he starts with his spiel. Then he'll look at Tara like he's Mother Teresa and she's some orphan child he picked up off the streets of Calcutta.

Deep inside, Tara doubts Sameer the Software Engineer knows anything about compassion. If he did, he wouldn't have spent half of their year-long relationship droning on about combustion engines or programming codes to her.

She takes another deep, desperate drag of her cigarette before babbling, 'I mean ... yes, of course, you're nice. You're great. I just don't think we're right for each other.'

Sameer lets out a strangled moan on the other end. After a long silence, as he presumably collects his thoughts, his tone gets uglier. 'Look, I get it. I am not like those guys in your novels. I don't wear leather jackets and ride bikes. That's what you want, right? Apart from werewolves and vampires?'

'That's not fair!' Tara argues, 'I just want passion, mystery, excitement. We're missing ... that spark.'

Sameer sounds snarky now. 'You mean, I don't make your "triangle quiver". For God's sake, what we have is real, Tara. A mature relationship. I've given you love, kindness, understanding ... I thought you wanted a good guy for a change?'

Sameer's voice fades as a black box that Tara likes to keep suppressed deep inside the crevices of her mind rattles. Neatly folded and arranged inside it are parts of herself that she'd hurriedly sawed off, not too long ago. The beast she once loved snarls, *But good guys are too boring for Tara Tandon, aren't they? Yeah, she likes them dark and dirty. After all, what's pleasure without a little bit of pain?*

Tara takes a deep breath, banishing the voice to the back of her mind to focus on Sameer. '... and by the way, everyone's right about your books on social media,' he's saying, going for the jugular. 'They are tacky. And they're setting women back by a hundred years. You're right. We're not the right fit. You don't deserve "nice"!'

He hangs up.

Tara rearranges her frenzied fringe. *Need to get rid of this stupid thing*, she thinks.

She fiddles with it, looking in the barely reflective black glass door of the shady pub. Slanting across her face, the sweep of hair was meant to compensate for her unflattering left profile, but she loathes the way it reflects her mood. On happy days, the strands point euphorically everywhere. But right now, they are sad and droopy, like she's feeling on the inside.

She has paired her short yellow skirt with a plain black sleeveless crop top, and tied her usually unruly, curly hair into a bun at the back of her head. She glares at her hazy, dishevelled, slutty reflection. But that's been her style for the past few years, hasn't it? The skimpier or shorter, more deep-cut or see-through, the better.

Tara dresses like she has something to prove.

The box rattles again, the beast whispering: *But she's still a part of you, isn't she? Fat Tara. No matter how tightly you bind and gag her, or which dark corner of your mind you shove her into – she'll always find her way back to the fore.*

Like the curve bulging out from under the waistband of Tara's skirt right now. *Lemme out, Tara, lemme oooooout*, the beast squeaks at a high pitch, before letting out a series of porcine grunts. She pulls up the fabric quickly and runs her hand down her sides once again to make sure it's all smooth.

She despises her face just as much as her body, so she likes to smother her eyelids with dark liner and kajal, drawing attention away from her ridiculously round nose and somewhat chubby cheeks. Her lips – not too big, not too small – are always drenched in wet, nude-coloured lipstick. They're the only part of her body she doesn't entirely hate, so she leaves them alone for the most part. Her ears are another story though – big, pointy, elfish. Tara loathes them so much she's pierced them at least ten times, as though punishing them by driving little heart- and snake-shaped studs into the cartilage; with silver and gold rings lining her lobes from top to bottom.

She heads inside and finally plonks herself down next to Ahana, grabbing her Long Island iced tea and inhaling it in one go.

Ahana motions to the server for another. 'Are you sure you want to end it? He is—'

'Don't you *dare* say the word "nice".'

'I liked him,' she shrugs.

Of course she does. Ahana is the sensible one. Miss I'll-be-a-partner-at-my-firm-any-day-now, Miss I'm-getting-married-to-my-college-boyfriend. Tara eyes her best friend with a slight hint of resentment. Ahana's slicked-back hair, her hands dainty and fingernails sharp with white French tips from a fresh manicure, her tailored cream just-out-of-office suit with matching Manolo Blahnik pumps, all scream 'I have it so fucking together'. It's amazing how she always smells expensive and fruity, how her sharp, angular face always looks fresh and dewy. She radiates inner peace – the kind you can't emulate with makeup.

But there's a slight furrow in her usually smooth forehead now, as she regards Tara with concern. 'You're okay, right?'

It's Tara's turn to shrug, as she gives Ahana a weak smile. 'I mean, I'm sure Twitter will find someone new to hate soon. And the publishers are still on board, as long as I make my next book more "politically correct".' Tara almost gags at the last two words.

The truth is that her abrupt fall from grace has left her shaken. There was a time when she'd been hyped as 'the next best thing' in desi romance and celebrated for 'fearlessly exploring women's deepest desires'. Her books, labelled 'risqué' rather than 'regressive', had rapidly climbed up bestseller lists, garnering a devoted following.

But something seems to have changed post the Wild Nights with the Werewolf series.

From the very beginning, Waris the Werewolf had rubbed everyone the wrong way. They hated all the things Tara loved about him: the fact that he was cold, cruel and callous before Laila melted his icy exterior and tamed and transformed him. Yes, he was alpha and a bit overprotective and aggressive, but that's to be expected from a werewolf, isn't it?

So she had blamed the criticism on the over-sensitive and much-too-politically-correct climate online. But it got worse, much worse, with the fourth instalment – *The Wolf's Captive.*

She wonders which was the straw that broke the camel's back. Was it when Waris abducted Laila? Or when he held her captive in a cave for weeks? Perhaps it was when he coerced her to marry him (as per his werewolf clan's long-standing tradition of forced weddings). Or was it the consummation of their wedding, that even Tara had to admit, was a tad too rough (even though Laila didn't seem to mind)?

Tara also wonders what all of this says about her, especially when one considers the fact that this was the first and only time that she had been unflinchingly honest and uncensored about her own desires in a book?

A group of twenty-something women walks by, whispering to each other as they shoot glances at Tara. It sends her right over the edge.

'Yes, it's me. The girl who killed feminism!' Tara shrieks. Doing her best Chucky impression, she flashes them a manic smile, punctuating her words with a series of jerky stabs with her fork in the air.

'We just ... we were just admiring your outfit,' one of the girls squeaks before they hurry away from her.

Ahana shoots her a knowing look. 'Forget the book, I'm worried about you.'

'I'm fine,' Tara rolls her eyes.

'You've lost so much weight, you're drinking way too much ... the last time I saw you like this—'

Tara screws her eyes shut, as the box in her brain begins to shake, letting out hideous creaks and groans. Thankfully, Ahana knows better than to complete her sentence. She just lets the words hang in the air, allowing their meaning to marinate and settle deep inside Tara's bones.

'Like I said, I'm absolutely fine,' she says, putting on her brightest, fakest smile. Luckily, Ahana's fiancé

Dheeraj saunters in at that exact moment, putting an end to the conversation.

Good ol' floppy-haired, always-smiling Dheeraj, dressed in a black shirt with cream pants to colour-coordinate with Ahana. Together, he and Ahana make the most well-adjusted couple. Even *Shaadi.com* and Seema Aunty from Netflix India couldn't have engineered a match this perfect on paper. They're both the same kind of good-looking and the same kind of successful, with the same kind of dad and mom humour. They finish each other's food and sentences, and call the other their best friend. Their combined confusion over Tara's romantic choices or those of the characters in her books is no wonder.

But they never give up on her. Even now, Dheeraj starts a conversation about setting her up with one of their lawyer friends.

And so, she abandons them, tired of being treated like a ticking bomb or a perpetual work-in-progress, heading to the dance floor and letting the crowd swallow her. At some point, Ahana and Dheeraj join her, though they soon head back to the table. Tara, however, continues to drink and dance for hours, till her feet hurt. Till the house lights come on. Till they start blaring the Bruno Mars song they play when they want everyone to leave.

The crowded room – clogged to the point of being a fire hazard – spins. The party's over, Tara can tell by how the stale air hits her. Its entrails are visible everywhere on the dance floor – cigarette butts and sticky beer stains; sweat-streaked faces bleeding makeup.

She's so disgustingly drunk, she can barely stand straight. But she's not ready to go home. The loneliness and hangover are sure to hit her ahead of schedule.

Finally, she spots Ahana and Dheeraj from the corner of her eye. They're flashing their phones at her, mouthing, 'It's 3 fucking a.m.' The music is still playing in her head.

I'm too hot (hot damn)
Call the police and the fireman
I'm too hot (hot damn)
Make a dragon wanna retire, man
I'm too hot (hot damn)

She yell-sings the words, trying to entice them back to the dance floor. Ahana throws up her hands in frustration, her eyes burning with a 'fuck you, Tara'.

That's when she spots him, making his way Moses-style through the crowd. Yelling the lyrics back at her.

She's too drunk to remember his name. But she vaguely remembers what Ahana used to call him. STD? Something like that. Something to do with how he's made his way across her entire friend circle and friends-of-friends circle like a venereal disease. 'How about you hook me up with one of your hot friends?' he asks her, every single time they meet.

'Porcine' was how someone had once described him. Something to do with the alignment of his nostrils, how his face was round and pink, how the neck ended before it began.

Still, he isn't ugly. Not at all. He is sort of cute, even, in a Jimmy Fallon kind of way. Tonight, sort of cute will do. Besides, STD clearly knows how to party and roll perfect joints.

He's never hit on Tara before – just her friends and friends-of-friends-of-friends – but right now he is grinding against her with a certain audacity. There's a smile of relief on his face, pleased that she's allowing this. Tara can tell he doesn't want to go home alone either.

She's glad they have that in common, besides their obvious love for 'Uptown Funk'.

As he leads Tara out of the club, Ahana tries yanking her away from his grip. 'Dude, what are you doing? You hate Herpes!'

Right. That's what they call him – Herpes.

Tara waves her friend off with a slurry, incomprehensible, 'Don'tworryabout meyo! Igotthis!', before disappearing into his red, second-hand Alto.

He's good in the sheets – gotta give Herpes that.

Tara rolls over on his bed – which is really just a *gadda* on the floor, covered with a psychedelic mandala bedsheet – and takes in her surroundings. The walls of his house are white and bare, as though deliberately stripped of personality. It's like he's a millennial monk who only needs a lava lamp and a PS4 to survive.

Stoned, slightly hungover and basking in post-coital oxytocin, Tara entertains the possibility – just for a second – that there might be more to this, to him and her. Except she doesn't stop there, of course. She lets her train of thought chug away from her, as usual; running off the tracks, steam billowing, passengers screaming ... hurtling all the way to Crazy Town. Choo choo!

You were right here. I just never saw you.

The Harry to my Sally!

We have so much in common, like 'Uptown Funk' and ... this terrible loneliness? Don't we? Don't we?!

Hear me out, Herpes! Maybe you could be my future husband.

Pathetic, needy and hungry.

It's when Herpes starts talking that Tara slams back into herself, alarm bells ringing through her body, fluttery red flags replacing the butterflies in her stomach. 'You lost a lotta weight recently, right?'

'It's been a couple of years, actually.'

'Yeah, I could tell from the sex, you know?'

'You could tell from the *sex*?'

'Yeah, chubby girls are different in the sack. They're, like ... pleasers.'

'What are the skinny girls like?' The whole thing's gross but part of Tara is curious.

'Self-conscious. Low energy, you know, because they barely eat. They hold back. That's why I prefer the chubby ones any day.'

Each time he says 'chubby', Tara winces. She wishes he would stop talking. With every word, she envisions the two-year-old boy from *Honey, I Blew Up the Kid* ruthlessly disassembling her train of he-could-be-the-one thoughts.

But he just rambles on. 'I dated a model once, and like, it made me realize, Ahana – sorry, *Tara* – deep down, they're just like the rest of us.'

I'm sorry, 'us'?

'Hot people just want to be seen, you know? All her life, this model felt objectified, and I think all she ever wanted was to be more than a body to men. She'd tell me, "I love how you just listen". No one ever really listened to what she was saying. No one valued her brain.'

'Right. So how did it end?'

'I mean, she *did* talk a lot.'

'Of course.'

'So, how's the new book coming along?'

'Well, it's on hold. I need to clear my head, I guess.'

'The elusive muse and all, right? I mean, not that I get all that stuff about werewolves, no offence. I read bits and pieces of your last one. Pretty dark and weird. I had always pegged you for a feminist.'

'Well, I *am* a feminist.'

He laughs at that.

Tara feels belatedly violated, as if he has given herpes to her soul.

'You could be a good writer, you know? Like, there's something in there. I saw flashes of it,' he drones on like some literary critic.

Shut up. Shut up. Shut up.

Tara had forgotten just how much Herpes loved to play the 'intellectual', name-dropping Kerouac and Hemingway in conversations, randomly segueing into the symbolism in a Bergman film or the choreography in a Kurosawa one to show off his knowledge of world cinema. He saw himself as a real Renaissance man who could talk about quantum physics while strumming Nirvana tunes on his guitar. But Tara always suspected that it was a front, a shell personality he had built solely to persuade more women into his bed.

'I dated this writer,' he continues, 'But she was, like, more on the literary side? Very Sylvia Plath meets Virginia Woolf. She had some demons. I see some similar demons in you. You just need to channel them, I guess.'

Tara can't sleep the next night. Her mind is stuck on Herpes' words, turning them over and over. '*I see some similar demons in you. You just need to channel them, I guess.*' His voice so casual when he said it. The box she had locked so tight, for so long, begins to rattle – its contents spilling into her dreams when she finally falls asleep.

The midnight-coloured beast from the cover of Wild Nights with the Werewolf *is crouched before her, snarling and spitting, ears pinned to the sides of its head.*

Slitted amber eyes boring into hers, it asks in a deep, gravelly and familiar voice, 'What are you so afraid of, my love?' Its voice turns even deeper, more seductive, as it adds, 'You want this, you know you do.'

In a heartbeat, it closes the distance between them, taking her arm in a possessive, vice-like grip.

Her fearful whimpers barely mask her desire, as one of its sharp yellow claws digs into her arm, drawing first blood.

2

'You're an hour late,' says her agent Vikram, as Tara walks into the bistro in Saket's Select Citywalk Mall.

The place is fashioned after a train station. A psychedelic weighing machine on her right triggers flashbacks of traumatic train rides. The servers are dressed as coolies, while the booths look like bogies with fake windows opening to watercolour fields.

'Sorry. I've just been struggling with sleep lately. Been having the most vivid nightmares,' she mumbles, sliding into the booth across from him. 'Wow, I hate this place,' she switches the topic instantly to rid her brain of the beast's image. 'Why can't restaurants just be restaurants?'

'You do look like a ... trainwreck,' Vik quips, peering at her from over his menu with a self-congratulatory grin. When his pun falls flat, his eyes scan her untamed curls, baggy, rumpled T-shirt and jeans. Her face is uncharacteristically bare of any makeup too.

'I can't tell if this is a new style statement or a cry for help,' he continues, still grinning, though his own T-shirt and jeans mirror hers. Except his white tee doesn't have ketchup stains on it, and his jeans are ripped in a way that's more deliberate and stylish. His salt-and-pepper hair is sculpted impeccably into a gelled tower of pouf. His Yeezy sneakers alone are worth the advance on her last book.

'Well, at least it isn't screaming "mid-life crisis" like yours,' she says with a saccharine smile, before turning her attention to the menu, suddenly feeling ravenous.

'New fragrance, too. I smell hints of despair and, wow, weed,' he tsks-tsks, with a shake of his head. 'Professionalism isn't really your strong suit, Tara.'

She ignores him, motioning to the server to call him over. 'Chocolate milkshake, burger, large fries.'

'Just a cold coffee. Thank you,' Vik says, already messing with her brain. Great, now he'll delicately sip on his coffee while she dives into full-throttle, eat-my-feelings mode.

He reminds her of the bitchy girls in school – the queen bees, the bullies, the fat-shamers. But even they weren't as skilled at mind games as Vik.

Determined not to let him get to her, she keeps the forced smile plastered on her face as she tells the server, 'I'll also have a sundae at the end.'

Might as well give him a good show.

That's why he's here anyway – to make her feel like shit with his version of a pep talk. He does this each time her writer's block goes on for too long. She'd hate him for it if it didn't somehow work.

'At least you're miserable, which is good,' he begins. 'You write like crap when you're happy.'

'Yup. I know.' Tara shrugs.

'You *are* writing, aren't you?' he probes. He is staring at her in that way job interviewers do, impregnating their pauses, waiting for the candidate to flinch, using their 'ahems' as bait. But Tara doesn't break a sweat, matching his stare as she says, 'Yes. I've written Chapter 1.'

It's a white lie. So far, she's only written the words 'Chapter 1' in a Word doc.

Her burger arrives – a delicious porky abomination, with several layers of meat interspaced with sauce. She contemplates how to eat it gracefully, before giving up and shoving it in her mouth. Ketchup, mayo and mustard drip down her chin, mixing with the older ketchup stains on her shirt.

'I have never seen someone eat a burger in such an unhinged manner,' Vik comments, looking away in disgust.

'Sorry, it's a coping mechanism,' Tara says through a mouthful. 'It's how I emotionally regulate myself, and deal with all the ... trolling.'

'Right. Also, please stop dating shitty men.'

'Which shitty men?'

He turns his gaze towards the fake window on the wall, addressing the watercolour fields because he still can't look at the crime scene unfolding on her plate. 'I saw him on your stories. Not worth your time. You're better than these loser fuckboys.'

'Thanks,' she mumbles.

'Besides, when you date shitty men, you write shitty men,' he says, circling back to business.

Tara rolls her eyes and shoves some fries into her mouth. He's right, of course. For all of Vik's bitchiness, she is grateful for their symbiotic, albeit slightly sadomasochistic, relationship. It's dysfunctional, sure, but effective. He champions her, tears her down, then builds her back up only to rip her apart again ... but it works.

'So, what's Chapter 1 about anyway?' He motions to the server to get Tara a box of tissues.

'It's a work in progress,' she says. 'It's hard to focus, with everyone writing my career obituary on social media.'

'At least Rhino still wants you – as long as you take the toxicity down a notch.'

'You mean make Waris a chocolate boy? He's a werewolf, Vik. I can't do that to him.'

He looks exasperated. 'Come on, Tara. All these

guys want is heaving, happy bosoms. You can write that stuff in your sleep.'

She sets down the burger and wipes her mouth with her shirt, just to see him flinch again. 'You know I don't like it when you make a joke out of what I do. Throbbing manhoods and quivering triangles apart, these books mean something to women. They really helped me through my teens. They're an escape and, some might say, the last bastion of female fantasy!'

'Oh, come on. You write smut, Tara!' Vik balks at her incredulously. 'Since when do you take yourself so seriously? If anything, I am the only one protecting this so-called bastion of female fantasy. A little appreciation wouldn't hurt!'

'Sanitizing my books, making them what the publishers want ... it feels *wrong*, like a disservice to my readers. And if I can't write another *Wild Nights with the Werewolf*, where does that leave me—'

'Lucky for you, you have a month to figure it out!' he says, cutting her impassioned speech short. 'Anyway, I'd love to stay and watch you dislocate your jaw trying to finish that burger. But I have errands to run.'

He steps out, leaving Tara to watch the slithering, frenetic shoal of happy, shiny, glossy people with somewhere to go absorb his happy, shiny, glossy self.

Tara gets home and makes herself a large pot of coffee. With a deep breath, she opens the Word doc on her Mac, and pops a piece of nicotine gum into her mouth. She chews rabidly, ignoring the chaos in her rented Vasant Kunj apartment a la 'A Hovel of One's Own'.

Plants lifelessly droop in their unwatered pots, which double up as dustbins. She sits on her unmade bed, using a pillow and a balled-up blanket as an impromptu desk. A pile of her unsold books is stacked against one of the ugly mustard-coloured walls, while the other has a pin-up board that's plastered with covers of Victorian bodice rippers – a shrine to all the dysfunctional romances that have shaped her writing. Each features a variation of the same archetype: the Bewitching Rake, the Wandering Wolf, the Philandering Count, the Reckless Viscount – shirtless and clutching catatonic semi-clad women on the brink of orgasm.

Tara can't seem to conjure up any words today. She silently stares at her laptop until the screen goes dark, shuddering at her own reflection – spotty, dark-circled, hair like a bird's nest – staring back at her.

She can't help but recall Ahana's worried words from last night, and her own disturbing dream of the beast taunting her. It chuckles in her head now, *Just give up, Tara. You're not just a talentless hack, but an emotionally damaged one at that.*

Shaking off the negativity, Tara finishes her coffee and reawakens her laptop.

'Chapter 1'. The desolate words mock her from the screen. Tara glares back at them till they blur into foggy squiggles. Minutes later, hypnotized by her own lack of productivity, she finds herself on Twitter, masochistically curious to see what the trolls are saying today.

She's been tagged over hundred times in a bizarre article titled 'Russian Tourist's Tragic Death Gets Plot Twist With Werewolf Killer Theory'.

She clicks on it to find a cheerful photograph of the twenty-three-year-old blond woman named Oksana Petrova, who was visiting Goa for a yoga teacher training course, next to the beach where her body was discovered. The article adds that she was found washed up on the shore with her throat ripped out. The Goa police initially thought a wild animal had attacked her because of the bite marks on her body. However, at least five eyewitnesses had sworn to have seen a strange 'wolf-like' creature on the beach the same night, walking on two legs – just like a man.

This wasn't the first such incident; three months prior, the body of an Israeli woman, Sofiya Galil, who also came down to Goa to learn yoga, was found underneath a cliff on the same beach, impaled on a rock, carrying similar wounds to the other victim.

Scrolling down, Tara sees they've even included

a sketch of said perpetrator – a black *Hound of the Baskervilles*-like creature standing on its hind legs, with blazing yellow eyes piercing through the page.

She glances through the comments accompanying the article:

'This murderer is right out of a @TaraT novel.'

'Hey @TaraT, come and get yo boy, Waris!'

'The Goan police have to be smoking the same stuff as @TaraT!'

As she mutes and blocks each of the commenters, Tara can feel the beginnings of an idea form in her brain.

Instead of channelling her demons, like Herpes had said, maybe it's time she exorcizes herself.

She knows what she needs to do. *Start afresh.*

Tara begins untacking all the romance posters from her pin-up board, gathering them into a pile on the balcony. There, she lights a cigarette, taking a deep, dramatic drag before flicking it onto the heap. She watches as the fire licks at her heroes and heroines, distorting their conjoined groins, before making its way to their perfect abs, swelling breasts and faces frozen in half-moans, slowly reducing them all to ash.

By evening, the board is transformed. A printout of the *Hound of the Baskervilles* creature has taken centre stage, flanked by headshots of its two victims, a sticky note detailing their backgrounds and all the clues related to the murder.

The beast visits her again in her dreams that night.

They're alone in a cave, somewhere dark and deep. All Tara can see are its yellow eyes, shining in mid-air. Its growls, low and guttural, echo off the walls.

Slowly but surely, her eyes make out the shape of the terrifying creature crawling towards her. There's a hyena-like grin on its face now, both ferocious and mocking.

'Let me take a bite of you,' the beast teases and implores, as its mouth drips drool, its eyes glittering with hunger.

A hunger ... for Tara.

Despite the fear slowly paralyzing every inch of her body, Tara can't help but be drawn to the beast. It looks at her like no other man has ever looked at her before. As though, despite all her flaws, it wants to possess her in a way no one else has ever wanted to. Like it wants to claim her flesh and tendons and bones and soul for itself.

And Tara's so grateful it does. She wants to give herself up to it, so badly.

But she's afraid. Not about the fact that it will hurt, but that the beast won't like how she tastes. What if she's too bitter or sour? What if she can't live up to the other girls it has eaten before? Girls who were born sweeter, softer, naturally delicious.

Tara feels a desperate urge to season herself before the beast does whatever it plans to do with her. To sprinkle herself with salt and pepper, dip herself in exotic herbs, turn herself into a flavour that it will never forget.

But the creature looks like it's in no mood to wait, so she ends up offering her arm to it, nervously.

It nibbles tentatively, then gnaws hungrily. She delights in the noises it makes – little growls and groans of pleasure. She finds herself getting wet at the sight of her flesh being ripped away, her soft tissues spilling out, the way her shining white bone glistens underneath.

'You taste exquisite,' the beast whispers, moaning in satisfaction. And Tara feels her heart dance in her ribcage. 'Better than I had imagined in my head. I could eat you all night, in fact. But I won't.

'Because I want to savour you, Tara.'

Those words make Tara's head and body explode into white, hot streaks of pleasure. She trembles uncontrollably with the knowledge that it's going to rip her apart.

And all she wants is more, more, more ...

3

Werewolves aren't real, of course. Tara *knew* that, even as she booked her tickets to Goa.

But boy, does sub-inspector Prakash 'Sunny' Cordeiro make a convincing case. Tara had contacted him after learning he was suspended for allegedly leaking the much-trolled werewolf sketch to the press. Fortunately, he was quite eager to speak to her, seeing as how his colleagues refused to be more broad-minded about this case.

'*Hypothetically speaking, even if werewolves were real, Goa would not be their "natural habitat", Sunny*,' he mimics one of his superiors now. '*Arre*, I know that, man. But we get lakhs of tourists flying in every year, you think one couldn't sneak in among them?'

The three-month suspension is looking good on Sunny. He's wearing swim shorts patterned with coconut trees and multicoloured waves and has chosen to forego his shirt. Tara's eyes skim over his dark body, lean yet still muscular – the kind that wasn't crafted from lifting and protein shakes, but a physically demanding job and swimming in the ocean – before settling on his face: tiny, beady eyes, a hawkish nose and thin lips with a Seventies Bollywood villain-style moustache framing them. With his sunglasses perched atop his head, a Kingfisher in his hand, he looks oddly relaxed.

They're at a shack on Anjuna Beach – the scene of the crime that doesn't really look like a scene of the crime. Just one month after the fatal attack, it's business as usual. The beach is overflowing with tourists of various nationalities.

'What is this interview for, by the way?' he asks her now. He glances at her from head to toe, taking in her multiple piercings, white crochet crop top and denim microshorts. She knows that she has overdone her makeup in an effort to hide the bags and shadows under her eyes, thanks to all the recent crying spells and late nights spent scrolling through a barrage of hateful tweets. However, the relentless heat is now making her concealer and mascara bleed and clot, while the humidity has expanded her curly hair to twice its size

'Let me warn you, this creature is nothing like in your books. Sexy, with six-pack abs and all. This is serious business.'

'I know.' Tara feels her face redden at his tone. 'I am trying to do something different this time. Like ... non-fiction.'

She takes a delicate sip of her Cabo and Diet Coke while he ponders over her words. 'Okay, but just don't name me. I don't want any more trouble.'

She nods, noticing how seamlessly Sunny fits in at the 'Shakti Shack'. Inside the rickety structure cobbled together from bamboo sticks and wood, the air is heavy with the smell of marijuana. It doesn't seem to bother the cop. In fact, he seems to be vibing with the soft reggae tunes playing in the background.

The place is a typical hippy, touristy set-up – indistinguishable from all the other shacks lining the shore. Thatched roof, cane furniture, trippy posters everywhere. Serving as the *pièce de résistance* is a larger-than-life psychedelic mural of Lord Shiva's face, beaming down at the mostly white patrons.

Sunny's currently talking to the server in Konkani, seemingly ordering half the dishes on the menu. Once done, he switches to English for Tara's benefit.

'So, Miguel, seen any *lobisomem* on the beaches lately?' he asks the server, who grins. Sunny turns to Tara, explaining, 'Lobisomem is—'

'Portuguese for werewolf,' Tara interjects. 'I know. Go on.'

The server continues to smile shyly at Sunny, 'What man, *anything*!'

Sunny refuses to back down. 'You think we are joking? Five people saw it, Miguel.'

'No offence, sir, but tourists see all sorts of things after a few beers. There is a wild dog that hangs around here from time to time. Pretty big. But from what I can tell, it has a liking for beef stew, not pretty white women,' the server shrugs, before heading back to the kitchen.

He returns twenty minutes later with a tray overflowing with squid recheado, pork sorpotel and chicken xacuti with poiees and parboiled rice.

'See, even my department agrees that the bite marks on the victim are very unusual. They are looking for either an unidentified animal or a non-standard weapon,' Sunny says in between mouthfuls of sorpotel.

Then, he slams a printout on the table.

It's a picture of the victim, Oksana, fresh after the attack. Half her face has been ripped off and chewed to the bone, while the other half is covered in gruesome slashes. But it's the one remaining eye, dangling from the socket, which causes Tara to almost throw up all the squid she'd inhaled seconds ago.

'Some warning would have been nice,' she grimaces.

'Sorry,' Sunny says hastily, before pulling her focus back to the picture, 'You tell me, madam, what human would do this?'

'This is ... horrible,' Tara cries, pushing her food aside as she studies the bites and lacerations on the victim's body. Every single part of Oksana has been mauled beyond recognition.

'We've been working with the Forest Department, but still can't find any identifiable DNA – animal or human – on the site. The bite and paw marks are similar to a wolf's, but have a much larger diameter.'

Tara chews on her lower lip, still on the fence. 'What if it is just that – a large wolf?'

He shakes his head. 'That's next to impossible. Firstly, there are no wolves in Goa – let alone one that is seven feet tall. And whatever attacked this poor woman had too much physical strength. It ripped her muscles apart, shattered her ribs ...

'But there's something else, something that proves this was no ordinary wolf. The post-mortem shows signs of struggle.' Sunny starts enacting the victim's last moments. 'She must have fought back like this,' he holds his hands out and paws at the air. 'Then the attacker grabbed her and slammed her head against the rock.' He grabs a piece of bread and whacks the plate over and over with it, until Tara has zero appetite left. 'You see the bite marks on her back and shoulder? It all means only one thing ...'

'What?' Tara asks, confused.

'A bipedal creature, madam ... whatever did this can walk, run and even use its hands like a human.'

She chews on that for a moment, before asking him, 'Can I keep this picture?'

Sunny nods, continuing, 'I spoke to the family that saw it. They are so scared, they have hardly slept since that night.'

'I mean ... it *was* late at night,' Tara argues, 'The beach wouldn't have been well-lit either. If someone saw something, they could convince the others too. Before you know it, everyone's seeing a werewolf!'

'Ah! But there is one twist – they weren't the first to see this creature.'

Tara's ears perk up at that. 'Really?'

'There have been sightings on Morjim and Arambol beaches, too. For years, in fact. The Russian community is sure there is a *wilkołak* among them. That is—'

'A shape-shifting figure from Slavic mythology, similar to the werewolf,' Tara interjects again. 'Waris ... you know, the character in my book, he had a wilkołak brother, so I know a thing or two about them.'

'Right,' Sunny says, unimpressed by her knowledge of werewolves. 'Neither the police nor the locals took these rumours seriously before – you know how these foreigners are, with all their crystals, chakras, third eyes and all. But with more eyewitnesses popping up ...'

Tara nods. 'Now that you mention it, I was researching both the victims. They belonged to the same yoga community – "Bliss". Which is primarily made up of Russians too. You think there's a link here?'

'Yes, we had been looking into that as well. Bliss certainly has a reputation here ... those women, I don't like the look of them.'

'What do you mean?'

'They all have the same smile,' he says with a shudder. 'They remind me of the antique dolls my grandmother used to collect. Big glassy eyes, ear-to-ear smiles. You'll know when you see it.'

'Any idea how I can get in touch with them?'

'Hmm ... that's tough. They don't usually let strangers walk into Bliss. But the night market might be a good place to start. They set up a stall there.'

'You wanna come along?'

'No, no ... they don't want me anywhere close to this case. I'm just going to enjoy my time off. Actually, I'd suggest you do the same, madam – enjoy the prawns, the beaches, the watersports and go home. You don't want to mess with Bliss or that thing, whatever the hell it is. Especially on a full moon night like this one.'

'So, you really, truly think this could be an actual werewolf?' Tara asks him, one last time.

Sunny grins, as he takes another sip of his beer. 'Until someone can prove otherwise.'

Tara grins back at him. His delusion is infectious.

Tara makes her way to the row of huts right behind Shakti Shack, propped up on stilts. They're basic, unimpressive, two-star rated on all websites. But this is all she can afford at the moment, seeing as she's spent most of her *Wild Nights* money, and probably won't be getting more any time soon. Inside, the room is dark, depressing and damp. But at least the balcony overlooks the ocean. It is the perfect vantage point for all the action unfolding on the beach.

She takes it all in now – the surfers and swimmers riding the waves, the joggers pounding the hot sand, parasailers dotting the sky and sun-bathers draped across deck chairs. Servers trudge from beach shacks to the sunbeds with frosty beers and sizzling seafood. Hawkers weave through the crowds, offering massages, tattoos and hair-braiding. Leaning forward, Tara catches a glimpse of the massive cliff framing the beach's far end. Sprawled atop it is an imposing structure that reminds her of a French Gothic castle.

Club Coyote.

Tara recognizes the infamous nightclub that's hated by authorities and locals alike for flouting SEZ regulations, and drug and sound laws. It is a stone's throw away from the scene of both murders and, according to some news reports, the authorities have been desperate to link the killings to it. It won't be easy, since the place is an institution – one of the last remnants of Goa's hippie era, a mecca for ravers across the world. She makes a mental note to check it out soon.

She drops her very light suitcase onto the floor. She hasn't packed much beyond a few changes of clothes. She'd left Delhi hurriedly in the dead of the night, since those were the cheapest tickets she could find. She had felt like a fugitive, running away from her whole life.

Most of the space in the suitcase is taken up by her investigation board. She props it up in one corner now, tacking the sketch that Sunny gave her next to the victims' smiling faces. She adds another sticky note underneath, on which she jots down all her new learnings, underlining the words 'Bipedal Attacker' five times.

Then, she hops on a call with Vik, filling him in on her morning, finishing with the dramatic proclamation, 'This is it ... my next book! Non-fiction about an actual werewolf.'

Vik sounds worried. 'I don't get it,' he tells her. 'Werewolves aren't real, Tara! Please tell me you know this.'

'It doesn't matter if they're real, Vik. Whatever this is – murderer, wild animal, or a combination of the two, I feel it's the best way to confront the image I have built in my head. To contrast the actual beast with my metaphorical ones.'

This only seems to confuse Vik further. 'Is it true crime? Because you're not a true crime writer. And this is not what Rhino wants. Do you really think this is the time to experiment, Tara? Why not just stick to what you know and do best – at least till the heat around *The Wolf's Captive* dies down?'

'This isn't about Rhino or the social media mob. This is about me,' she argues.

She hears Vik sigh, before he adds resignedly, 'Okay, go do your *Eat, Pray, Love*, "hunt a werewolf" thing. We can hash this out later. But for fuck's sake, be careful. Whatever this thing is – it sounds way worse than Waris.'

After a shower, Tara spends several minutes scrutinizing her reflection in the mirror, conducting her daily inventory of her flaws. Eyes – still puffy. Skin – especially dry from the heat and lack of hydration, moisturization or sleep. Pores – grotesquely enlarged. Body – seems a bit bigger lately, perhaps because she can't stop 'eating her feelings'. Hair – frizzy and out-of-control. Then she spends an hour trying to get rid of these defects with the help of cosmetics and a hair straightener. For a quick moment, she wonders if she should opt for an undercover outfit – something black and shapeless, maybe with a pair of shades and a hat – before changing into a bright blue strapless, body-hugging dress she bought at the beach. One last critical glance at her reflection, and she is ready to face the Saturday night market.

The informal marketplace was first introduced by foreign hippies, who settled here in the 1960s, to barter their belongings or crafts for essentials like food and clothing. Today, it's a kitschy, overcrowded tourist spot. Tara jostles through the sweaty crowd at the entrance to step inside a vast open ground, where over a hundred stalls are selling cheap beachwear, imported leather, turquoise, amethyst and quartz jewellery, the entire Indian pantheon of gods and goddesses carved from rock and wood, dreamcatchers, macrame hangings, psychedelic tapestries, didgeridoos, djembes, CDs and vinyl records of original Goan trance music, among other things. An entire side is taken up by the woo-woo lot. The fortune tellers, palmists, healers, Reikists. Tara gravitates towards them, squinting at the placards with indecipherable Russian words, until she finds what she is looking for.

Bliss. The word is accompanied by a minimalist logo showing a naked woman doing the downward dog.

As she approaches the counter, Tara sees four stunning women on the other side of it. Despite their wildly contrasting physical features – one's blonde and pale, the second red-haired and freckled, the third brunette and tanned, and the fourth dreadlocked and dark – they strike Tara as identical in their matching flowing white dresses and floral wreaths in their hair. They have similar bodies, too, the kind you can only achieve through rigorous workouts.

They also have the same smile, just like Sunny had said. Like someone had carefully carved it across their faces with a knife. It sends a chill down Tara's spine.

Still, she can't help but be drawn to them. A yellow, halo-like glow envelops them as they welcome Tara to the stall decorated in soft lavenders and muted pinks. It smells like heaven. A mix of freshly baked cookies and newly blossomed flowers. The counter is covered in baskets full of exotic herbs, incense, herbal oils, soap, candles and tea.

'It's all handmade,' the redhead tells Tara in a soft, husky voice.

'Really?' Tara smiles, watching the woman's delicate arms dance over the baskets. She suddenly feels so self-conscious among these slender women. It makes her want to claw her own plump arms off her body.

The beast rears its head again in her brain: *You're not like them. You'll never be anything like them.*

Tara picks up a bar of soap to sniff it, and her eyes fall on another basket filled with lockets, a purple flower encased in each.

Wolfsbane.

It's one of the oldest and most overdone werewolf tropes – one Tara refuses to include in her own books, even though she knows all about it. Now, she wonders if there is some truth to all the European folklore claiming wolfsbane can ward off werewolves or break their curse.

While its effect on werewolves might be debatable, the plant is pretty deadly for humans. It is shocking they're selling it in the open.

'Is this for the wilkołak?' Tara asks. 'I have heard that they spotted one around here.'

The redhead's eyes widen before she nods. She looks like she's dying to say something more, but is afraid. Tara takes a closer look, registering the purple crescents under the woman's eyes. There's an eerie expression in them, like that of a trapped animal.

'Did you know those women who were killed?' Tara prods anyway.

She senses a sudden chill in the air as a strikingly gorgeous woman joins them, wearing the same white flowing dress as the others. But she's thinner than the rest; her hair so blonde, it's almost white. Cropped till her shoulders, perhaps to draw attention to her spectacular collarbones. They are so sharp, they threaten to break through her skin and impale Tara's eyes. She's older than the other women in the group by a good ten years. Somewhere in her late thirties, Tara guesses.

She watches as the woman admonishes the redhead in stern Russian. The group falls silent, their eyes reflecting fear and subservience, smiles drooping for a split second.

Only then does she focus her searing gaze on Tara, who is struck by the strange colour of the woman's eyes – a translucent amber with just a slight hint of green.

'Why do you ask these questions of my girls?' she demands, snatching the locket back from Tara.

'I am working on a book. If I could just get a small interview ... it can be off the record, if you like ...'

She stares Tara up and down. Her voice is ice cold as she says, 'We have lost people close to us. Please don't come here and make a mockery of their deaths.'

Tara's cheeks grow hot, but she straightens her spine and plasters a sugary smile on her face before walking away. She passes a stall selling Bob Marley T-shirts, before moving on to one with an elaborate range of hookahs. She haggles half-heartedly over an orange *shisha*, but the whole while, she can't stop staring at the Bliss stall from the corner of her eye.

After an hour of faffing about, she gives up and walks defeatedly to her rental car. Just as she's about to get in, a voice calls out, 'Sorry, our mother – Ana – doesn't like us talking about the dead girls.'

She turns around to see that it's the redhead from Bliss. 'I'm Daria,' the woman says, awkwardly.

Tara smiles in response, 'Don't worry about it, I understand.'

She's about to turn back around when Daria adds, 'We don't know what happened to them. But I wish to.'

Tara leans against the car. 'Do you think it was a wilkołak?'

The woman looks around nervously, nods, then takes a large swig from the paper cup in her hand before saying, 'It visits us … sometimes. I have seen it.'

'Have you tried to tell the police?'

'Ana won't let me,' Daria says, adding, 'Oksana was good friend of mine. She came to Goa to learn yoga, like me. But then … bad company. Did too much drugs. Lost all money. Visa expired. Ana helped her get clean, earn money … same with Sofiya.'

She takes a long pause, as though searching for the right words in her limited English vocabulary. Then she continues, 'Ana is not bad … she helps us. But she doesn't like it when we leave.'

'What do you mean?'

'Too many secrets inside Bliss.'

'What about you? Have you ever wanted to leave?'

Tara sees something flicker in the woman's eyes, before she shrugs, 'Yeah. Sometimes.'

Then she extends her delicate arm towards Tara, unfurling each finger with nails painted a pretty seashell pink. There, in her palm, is the locket containing wolfsbane.

Tara offers her some money in return, but Daria shakes her head. 'Gift,' she says, turning to leave.

'Hey, wait! Where are you going?'

'Party. You want to come?'

Tara nods.

Daria offers her the paper cup, filled with a thick, foamy liquid. 'It's Bliss's specialty. You can finish.'

'Thanks,' Tara smiles, taking a large sip, and hopping onto Daria's rickety red scooty.

Daria drives fast and reckless, taking sharp turns into narrow inroads, until they have left civilization far behind. After twenty minutes or so, they reach a rocky, sandy stretch in the middle of nowhere. It's as far as the two-wheeler will go. They trudge through the sand; Daria dragging her scooty along with her, Tara wondering if she's made a mistake. She barely knows the woman. This doesn't feel safe. Besides, it's too dark and way past her bedtime ... but then she hears the faint echo of the beats. A dancing red light calls out to her from a distance.

They quicken their pace, until they finally reach a sign that reads 'Shiva Moon Party'.

A white man in orange robes with a pundit's *sikha* greets them with a serene smile. 'Welcome. Two hundred rupees ticket to go inside,' he says, in a heavy Russian accent.

'Talk about cultural appropriation,' Tara mutters under her breath, rolling her eyes as she hands him the money.

She walks into what looks like a cross between a fair and a circus. White tents pitched on sand house stalls selling food, clothes and trinkets. In the middle is a dance floor, with a dreadlocked and vampirically pale DJ presiding over it. Behind him is an LED screen, on which an otherworldly woman made up entirely of intricate neon patterns dances. She has three eyes that blink to the beat, and tentacles for hair that keep swaying to the rhythm. Every few minutes, she opens her mouth, revealing several maze-like psychedelic universes inside it. Tara watches, hypnotized.

And then the world explodes.

There are lights everywhere ... too many lights for comfort. A curtain of pink, blue and purple laser dots beams at her seductively before threatening to swallow her. It recedes before it can touch her – swirling, shaking and shimmying at her from a distance.

'Come back,' she whispers, mesmerized. As if in response, the coloured dots arrange themselves into a massive spider web, launching themselves at her feet and making her giggle.

She looks up at the sky, where the stars are dancing, too, in perfect coordination with the laser beams. Then, she's distracted by a kid eating fire and a woman twirling a flaming hula hoop.

She walks past fluorescent paintings and sculptures. In one, she sees a million eyes blinking at her. In another, she watches a mandala churn, bleeding orange and pink and green. Tara is sure she spends half an hour gawking at every single one, even though time is just a construct to her now.

'Having fun?' a voice says behind her.

It's Daria, but she's all elongated, and bobbing from side to side. Her voice sounds so far away, even though she's standing right in front of Tara.

'Is it working?' she asks from the same faraway place. Tara squints, hoping that will make Daria stop spinning like a mandala.

'What?'

'The drink,' Daria smiles.

'Wait, what?' Tara shakes her head, suddenly anxious with the realization that she's tripping right now. She's so high, in fact, that she can clearly see Daria's aura. A bright, sunny, yellow.

'Don't worry, it'll wear off soon. Just enjoy the ride,' Daria says, grabbing her hand and leading her to the dance floor. Closing her eyes, Tara focuses on the music that's slowly gaining tempo. She feels like she's on a rollercoaster ascending towards the peak, as a deep male voice talks about 'our infinite collective consciousness'. The DJ continues to gather momentum, and Tara finds herself swaying along with the crowd in anticipation. There's a magical moment of split-second silence, followed by the drop – and then an explosion of frenetic beats. Tara's body takes over from there. She dances till she's sweaty and out of breath.

When she opens her eyes, Daria's no longer beside her. She searches in the crowd, at every stall, amid the fire-breathers and revellers, but there's no sign of her. Panicking, Tara walks away from the party and towards the beach.

The ocean's never looked more dazzling. It is so beautiful that Daria starts to fade from her mind. Tara giggles as she dips her feet into the water, observing the large black waves rising in the distance. The rocks and the clouds are speaking to her in their native language. The sky is so friendly, ancient and wise, as it beams down at her. Another giggle rises in her throat. She feels like a toddler being watched over by the universe.

She speaks to it for what feels like hours, until they're interrupted by a scream.

'*Shhhhhh, Tara, listen*,' a cloud gently whispers to her.

Tara looks around frantically, her breath quickening as she takes in the eerie silence that surrounds her. The rocks have stopped whispering. The trees are no longer swaying. She can't feel the wind on her skin or hear the roar of the waves anymore.

No, the world is deathly still.

Tara looks at the ocean – dark, quiet, unmoving. A huge, towering wave, almost touching the sky, has stopped in its tracks. Despite its stillness, it feels sentient as it glares down at the miniscule Tara. A being that's hundreds of feet tall. Swollen, angry and ready to wash over her. She starts running away from it, across the dark and sandy expanse of the beach, realizing for the first time that she's all alone.

A feeling of helplessness dawns upon Tara, as she sprints past the empty shacks that look like a ghost of their former lively selves. She passes a row of boats, neatly laid out on the beach, hollow and upside down.

Then she hears it again. The same chilling scream, followed by animal grunts.

Instinctively, she ducks for cover under one of the boats, while looking around frantically for the source of the noise.

Finally, she notices two shapes in the darkness, far, far away. At first, she struggles to decipher what's happening. But once she focuses, her vision becomes superhuman, just like her other senses tonight. The scene gets clearer, brighter, louder, as though it were playing out on a movie screen.

A woman in a flowy white dress seems to be wrestling with a creature thrice her size. A creature she is no match against. Giant, muscled, hirsute – almost prehistoric in shape and size.

Tara recognizes the white dress flowing almost romantically in the wind. A flash of red.

Daria.

Tara watches as the bestial creature grips Daria by the waist with its massive hairy arms. Time slows down as it removes the hair from Daria's miniscule nape with its giant paw – a gesture that strikes her as oddly human, almost tender – before it sinks its fangs into her neck.

'No, no, no, no, *no*,' Tara whispers, slithering out from under the boat. She runs towards them, before collapsing onto the sand on all fours. A primal scream builds up in her throat, dying halfway to her lips when she realizes that Daria is no longer fighting back.

With her neck still caught in its jaw, Tara watches in horror as the monster jerks Daria around like a rag doll. It lets go and her body flies a few feet through the air before landing violently on the ground. There's no sound. Daria is clearly dead. Still, Tara watches as the creature rips her apart further with its sharp claws.

When it's satisfied with its kill, it abandons her limp body and pads across the sand on its hind legs. She watches it grab a Corona from a rock next to it, impossibly tiny in its paws. It gulps the beer down in seconds, before smashing the bottle to the ground.

Tara turns to escape before this thing sees her, only to hear a loud 'crunch'. She sees a broken branch under her foot. *Shit.*

The creature cocks up an ear, before turning around to look straight at her, their eyes locking for a heartbeat.

For as long as she lives, Tara knows she'll never forget the sight of this creature that seems to have crawled out of the depths of hell. Its eyes are a cruel and savage yellow. Its grin fanged, brutish and bloody.

This isn't a wolf, Tara realizes in that moment. No, it's the face of the devil.

She breaks into a sprint.

She runs till her feet ache; till her lungs are on fire.

Too bad she doesn't see that rock jutting out of the sand. Next thing she knows, she's falling to the ground, her head hitting something hard.

The world goes dark.

4

What followed is still a blur to Tara. When she had come to, a tall stranger, with the broadest shoulders she had ever seen, had been leaning over and flashing a bright light in her face. 'There's no concussion. Don't worry, you'll be fine,' he had said. She tries to recollect his scent now: woody, earthy, slightly musky.

He had carried her through the woods, reassuring her, 'You're okay. We're almost there,' his voice deep and soothing.

Sudden bright lights, loud noises – and then him laying her on something soft and velvety, stroking her head tenderly as she sobbed in his arms. His eyes had been a smoky grey, she recalls, the colour of the quiet before a storm.

More voices had joined them.

Tara ensconced in a sea of white as the Bliss women

had gathered beside her, the stranger disappearing behind them without so much as a goodbye.

Her guiding the group to Daria's dead body. Hearing their gut-wrenching cries as they had fallen in a heap around it.

'I saw what happened,' Tara had whimpered to them. 'It was the wilkołak.' She had recounted all that had happened.

But Ana had shut her down. 'You're high as a kite,' she had said doubtfully.

'We have to go to the police!' Tara had insisted. 'This thing is out there ... it's dangerous. I saw what it can do!'

'You can barely walk straight, and your pupils are blown out,' Ana had said pragmatically. 'All you will do is get yourself and the rest of us in trouble. Let us handle it. You should leave. You seeing it means you are in trouble.'

Tara remembers going back to the hotel at dawn, and sobbing to Ahana over the phone, who had begged her to come back home.

'Is this more important than your *life*?' she had demanded.

Probably not. But Tara had felt like a dog with a bone. She couldn't let go – not after what she had seen with her own two eyes. A werewolf, or the closest thing to it.

'You were high, Tara. What if you imagined the whole thing?'

She hadn't.

She spends the rest of the day locked up in her room, lying under the sheets with the curtains drawn. But it's hard to sleep with the drugs still in her system and the murder playing on loop in her head.

When sleep does arrive, it's restless and infested with nightmares.

Tara and the wilkołak are standing before a mirror, as he holds her the same way he held Daria.

The beast nuzzles her nape with its snout. She watches in the mirror as it bares its fangs, lightly grazing her tender skin. She shivers in anticipation.

'It could have been you tonight,' it says, in a voice deep and feral.

'I know.'

'It's almost like you wanted *it to be you.'*

'No, I didn't.'

'Liar.'

Tara winces as its teeth sink into her skin.

But the pain is soon gone, replaced by that perverse pleasure she craves.

With each bite, she relaxes further, giving into it.

'Come on, admit it,' the beast growls. 'It's your hunger that feeds mine.'

Tara wakes up to a chilling scream, reminiscent of Daria's last cries for help. Her heartbeat picks up as she leaves her bed and treads softly to the balcony.

She looks over the wooden railing, spotting two shapes just like the ones last night. A woman wrestling and straining against a beast. But as her eyes adjust to the moonlight, and the screams turn into moans, she realizes that she is unwittingly witnessing something entirely different.

There's a naked yet familiar blonde woman entwined with – not a beast – a very large, very muscular man on a beach chair.

It's Ana, Tara realizes, blushing.

And this isn't murder.

Judging from the look of it, this is something far more pleasurable.

Just as she's about to walk away, the man looks up. A knowing smile flashes across his face, his gaze pinning her to the spot.

Tara's face reddens as she watches him grab Ana's hair to elicit another feral moan, as they move to the same wild rhythm that's rough yet playful.

She feels something hot and hungry build up inside her. A mix of desire and envy so strong, she's almost afraid of it.

She knows she is intruding, but she can't look away from those eyes holding her own ... that perfect shade of smoky grey signalling the arrival of a storm.

5

Sunny's all wet and sandy from a fresh swim when Tara walks into Shakti Shack, wearing a large, grey, sack-like smock, and giant shades. He has two steaming plates of butter chicken and garlic naan in front of him. 'Comfort food for Delhiites, no?' he says with a smile.

She rolls her eyes, slightly offended by the stereotype, before devouring the food with a ferociousness that scares him.

'Are you okay?' he asks her, his voice reflecting deep concern as she takes off her shades to reveal her eyes, swollen and red from all the tears and the lack of sleep.

Tara waves him off with a 'Ya, ya. All good.'

That's when his concern turns from touching to condescending. 'I have to say, it was very stupid of you to take drugs from strangers,' he says, shaking his head like a disapproving aunty.

'I didn't *know* it was drugs,' she argues.

'It's all about having good reflexes,' he continues. 'For example, when you see a lobisomem, you run away from it. Not towards it!'

'What was I supposed to do? An innocent woman was being murdered!'

'So you wanted two innocent women murdered instead?'

Tara glowers at him.

He leans back. 'That Ana ... she's right. You can't go to the police station. Your eyewitness account is no good if you were high.'

'That's kind of why I called you. Maybe you can do something?'

'Arre, I already said I am off the case. *Kai ko* you're involving me? Anyway, even I am not sure if I really trust your version of events.'

'Okay, what if we put this werewolf thing aside for a bit? Before she died, Daria told me that Oksana, the one who was murdered last month, was trying to leave Bliss. Apparently, Ana wouldn't let her. And I could tell that Daria wanted out as well, before the same thing happened to her.'

Sunny doesn't reply. He takes a big swig of his Kingfisher, staring into the ocean.

But that doesn't deter Tara. 'I think you and your colleagues should look into Ana,' she addresses his disinterested side profile. 'There's something off about that woman. Have you noticed her eyes? They're yellow ... like a wolf's. Anyway, I'm planning to see her later this week.'

That grabs his attention. He turns away from the ocean to fix Tara with an incredulous stare. 'You're what?!'

'If you guys won't do anything, someone has to!'

He shakes his head, 'Thanks for telling me how to do my job. Great advice from someone who takes drugs from strangers. Meanwhile, here's *my* advice to you – stay away from Ana. We've been on her tail for all sorts of things. Drugs, prostitution, trafficking, financial fraud ... She's an expert criminal with the full support of the mafia. You are a romance writer with two-star ratings on Amazon. Who do you think will win this one?'

Tara crosses her arms in front of her chest in defiance.

Sunny's face grows serious. 'I mean it. Get over Ana and this wolf. Let the professionals handle it.'

Tara channels the same stubbornness she did with Ahana. 'But I *can't* let it go!'

Sunny's eyes narrow. 'Why does this sound like it is about more than just a book to you?'

She simply shrugs in response.

He leans over the table, shaking his head, 'It's as if you're looking for trouble.' Then he gets distracted as someone approaches them, face instantly souring.

'If it isn't Miss Peeping Tom …' a deep, velvet-smooth voice says from behind her. A voice that's incredibly familiar, as is the person's scent.

Tara turns around to find herself face to face with Mr Smoky Grey Eyes.

She's thankful her past two encounters with him happened at night, in the shadows. To be honest, even the drugs might have helped. She is in no way physically equipped to handle the sight of him in broad daylight, and without a shirt.

He has to be well over six feet tall, judging by the way he towers over everyone in the shack. The fact that he is shirtless also means that she has an ample view of the water droplets still clinging to his four – no wait … six-pack – abs, and the slight sprinkle of hair on his chest that narrows into a V before disappearing into the waistband of his wet, black swimming trunks.

'Hope you enjoyed the show last night,' he says, forcing her to look up at his face and then turn a bright shade of red. He almost seems amused by her discomfort.

She notices how he looks to be a strange mix of Goan and something more exotic; his dark, sunburnt skin clashing with his grey eyes. His shoulder-length hair perfectly hugs his broad, almost perfect face. Every feature is sharp, symmetrical and flawless, save for his nose, that's large and misshapen like it has been broken and bloodied one too many times.

As soon as he says the words, Tara braces herself for the onslaught of racy mental images from last night. *Him and Ana's rough, animal sex, all those moans ...*

'It was okay,' she shrugs, trying her best to play it cool. 'Though I suggest you take your show somewhere more private next time? Considering your girl's quite the screamer.'

His grin widens at that, dimples denting both his cheeks. He holds her gaze and whispers, 'Does that mean you're a quiet one?'

Tara can feel her palms getting sweaty, as she huffs, 'It means nothing of the sort.'

With a slight raise of an eyebrow, he looks at her again, and she finds herself trembling from the sheer violence of his stare. Lazy and unhurried, his gaze sears her from her toes to the top of her head, before burning into her eyes. She's suddenly all too aware of how unkempt she looks in her tragic, snot-coloured dress, without a smidge of makeup on her face. She runs a hand through her frizzy, knotted hair, feeling naked, all of her flaws on display, and struggles to form her next words. 'Anyway, I wanted to thank you for ... ummm ... saving my life that da—'

'No worries. I am glad I could help.'

Finally, he turns to Sunny, and Tara feels a sense of relief just being released from his gaze.

Something tells her the two men have already met. It's the way they are glowering at each other with a special hatred. Like two dogs guarding their territories.

'Noel,' Sunny addresses him, with a slight nod.

Noel. She rolls his name around her tongue, hating how good it feels.

'Sunny,' Noel replies.

'I was just telling Tara that there are dangerous animals in this town, and she should stay away from them,' Sunny says with a smile that she's only seen on apes on National Geographic. The ones who bare their teeth as a sign of aggression.

The dimples disappear from Noel's cheeks, as he returns Sunny's glare. 'I hear they pulled you off the murder case? Pity, since that lobisomem sketch was really your finest piece of work.'

That seems to get under Sunny's skin. 'If I were you, I'd be more worried about Coyote. Been hearing some whispers about a fresh raid,' he spits out.

That makes Noel smile. 'Awww, another one? Can't stay away, can they? Thanks for the heads-up though,' he says, leaving Sunny stewing.

Then he leans close to Tara, his lips almost grazing her ear as he whispers, 'See you around.'

As soon as he leaves, Tara releases the breath she didn't realize she had been holding. She slumps back gracelessly in her chair, almost sliding off it in the process. Sunny shoots her a dirty look. 'What's got into you?'

'Was I that obvious?' she asks, fanning herself with a napkin like a Victorian heroine.

He flutters his eyelashes, imitating her breathless '*thank you ... for saving my life*'.

She throws the napkin at him. 'Yeah, well, you were equally obvious. I was afraid you were going to tackle him to the ground or something.'

'Nah, I'd do much worse to him,' he replies with the same sour look on his face.

Tara ignores that, instead asking, 'So, *he* owns Coyote. That's the one on the cliff, right?'

'Exactly. You've managed to make some dangerous friends in just two days. Please be ca—'

Tara cuts him off, 'Careful. Yes, I get it!'

The moment she's back in her room, Tara dives back into her research.

She starts with Oksana's Instagram profile, scrolling to the bottom of the page, to 2016, the year she first arrived in Goa.

Blonde, blue-eyed, with her pale skin burnt red from too much time in the sun, Oksana is the quintessential Goan tourist in the first few pictures. Cartwheels on the beach, cocktails at shacks, sunrise hikes, sunset yoga, enthusiastic videos of her immersing herself in Indian culture – the food, the sights, the people ... there's nothing suspicious to be found. She looks happy.

But something changes in 2017. She drops off the grid completely till 2018, only to return in 2019 looking like an entirely different person. This 'new' Oksana is incredibly skinny. Worryingly so, with her cheeks hollowed out and her eyes sunken in. Unlike the previous pictures, where her shoulders were proudly pulled back and her back ramrod straight, she's now hunched over and withdrawn into a tight ball, like someone trying to hide in plain sight. Her face no longer glows like it used to. It's almost like her happiness has been slowly leached out of her. What's left is that trademark Bliss smile: lips parted too wide, eyes devoid of any expression.

Tara recalls Daria's words: '*She came to Goa for yoga, you see. But then ... bad company. Did too much drugs. Lost all money. Visa expired. Ana helped her get clean, earn money ...*'

In every picture that follows, Oksana's wearing the signature Bliss uniform: dresses like the ones Tara saw at the night market. She's surrounded by a bevy of women in the same clothing. 'Family', reads one caption in Russian. There are several pictures of her with Ana, too, calling her 'mother'. There's one particularly gushy write-up, describing how Ana took her in when her own family abandoned her.

Tara rolls her eyes. *Ugh, she makes this woman sound like Jesus or something.*

Still, there's something off about these pictures, though Tara can't quite put a finger on what that thing is. Life at Bliss looks idyllic. They grow their own organic produce, bake bread from scratch, weave and stitch and craft all kinds of products to earn money. True to the place's name, their days seem blissful; filled with yoga, healing and drum circles, meditation, music, and lots and lots of sisterly bonding.

Tara realizes what's off: It all looks completely inauthentic, just like the women's smiles. An elaborate hoax constructed for the world outside. There's a look in each one's eyes, that seems to cry, 'Save Me'.

She recalls Daria's words again: '*She doesn't like it when we leave ... too many secrets inside Bliss.*' Along with Sunny's: '*We've been on Ana's tail for all sorts of things. Drugs, prostitution, trafficking, financial fraud ... She's an expert criminal with the full support of the mafia.*'

One picture, in particular, catches Tara's eye. It's clearly from some kind of a ceremony. All the women are dancing in a perfect circle around a fire in a forest. Oksana has titled it 'Full Moon Therapy'.

Their Bliss smiles are missing in this picture. Instead, each woman seems to be grinning with pure ecstasy, their eyes wild with joy, like they've finally been allowed to be free.

It all goes downhill from that day for Oksana. With every successive picture, she seems to lose more weight, and curl up tighter into herself. Her last picture is a haunting one: There's shadows under her eyes, and a resigned look on her face. Like she knew what was coming.

That expression feels all too familiar to Tara. It was the same one she saw on Daria's face that night.

Tara calls it quits somewhere around midnight, crawling into bed with a promising beach read she bought at the airport. It's about a woman trying murder her own family and, within minutes, Tara finds herself completely engrossed.

It takes her a while to register the clicking noise at the door.

She ignores it, too comfortable under her sheets. It's not like she's expecting anyone. Besides, her book is just getting spicy, with the protagonist having killed her grandmother.

But the clicking doesn't stop. The sound is annoying enough to make Tara put her book aside, and stare at the door resentfully. It disappears for a few moments, only to be replaced by dull, repetitive thuds.

This makes her bolt upright, her heartbeat quickening.

Thud. Thud. Thud! It continues, each 'thud' louder, more ominous, followed by the rough and unsettling sound of claws scraping against the door's surface.

Tara stays deathly still, hoping whoever it is will take the message and leave. But the thuds only get more and more insistent. They're now accompanied by faint whimpering noises. It sounds like a dog begging to be let in.

She stands up and starts walking towards the door. As though sensing her footsteps, the creature lets out a long, piercing moan. She can hear it panting heavily as it slams the door, then scratches at it desperately.

She grabs a chair and places it under the knob, before bringing her ear to the door.

It starts growling.

She backs away, rushing to the phone and calling up the main desk. No answer.

The creature continues to claw at the door and growl. The sound is deep, guttural ... almost demonic.

She dials the main desk again, but no one picks up.

Whatever it is, it's throwing all its weight into the door now, threatening to knock it off its hinges.

It alternates between snarling ferociously and whimpering pathetically for several more minutes, slamming against the door. Then it lets out a long, bone-chilling howl, followed by silence.

It seems to have given up.

Finally, someone picks up the phone. 'Room service. How may I help you?'

Minutes later, Tara hears a human knock. 'There's nothing here, ma'am. We checked,' an apologetic employee tells her. 'It's probably one of the beach dogs. Do you have leftovers in your room?'

She nods.

'Ah, it must have smelt those. Don't worry, they're harmless. Just keep your doors shut.'

She gives him a small smile, and locks the door once he leaves, placing the chair under the knob again as added protection. Those growls had sounded far from harmless to her.

A part of her wonders if Ana was right. Is the wilkołak coming for her next?

6

Tara's coffee and croissant sit cold and forgotten at Shakti Shack. Her hands, still trembling from the previous night, light her second cigarette of the day. She wants to call Sunny to talk about last night's terrifying events, but she knows he'll only make her book her ticket back to Delhi.

To be fair, that would be the logical thing to do. In fact, most people – if they were to find themselves face to face with a horrifying creature – would do just that. They'd convince themselves that there was no such thing as a werewolf, and go back to living their normal lives. That's precisely what the police seem to be doing as well.

But not Tara. Things will never be normal for her, not after what she has seen. Going back would mean dishonouring the victims and leaving more women vulnerable to this all-too-real monster.

You self-righteous hypocrite, the beast in her head snarls. *Is it really about the victims or is it all just a sorry attempt to un-cancel yourself? You really think you'll defeat this monster and write the greatest true crime story of all time, don't you? For fuck's sake, Tara, you're not Truman Capote, you're straight-up delusional!* She lights another cigarette, trying to drown out her mental chatter. Then she looks around the shack, trying to anchor herself in her surroundings. That's when she spots him, two tables away from her.

Noel. Shirtless as usual, his abs on full display. In his hand is a book that he seems fully engrossed in. A book that she knows all too well.

The Wolf's Captive (Wild Nights With The Werewolf #4).

Ugh, she winces as he looks up, a slow grin spreading across his face.

Worse, he's coming over to her table. Tara looks around frantically for the nearest exit, but it's too late. As he gets closer, she continues sitting there, feeling like prey caught in a trap, wriggling helplessly, as the predator closes in. He does not take his eyes off her for even a second as he walks towards her, and she returns his gaze courageously, even though her face is burning like she has swallowed a whole ball of wasabi. She realizes she is still wearing the baggy old T-shirt and shorts she slept in last night, with her hair wrangled into a hapahazard bun on the top of her head. She had literally rolled out of the bed and into the shack this morning, desperate to be out in the sun and amidst a crowd of people, and away from the monster in her head or outside her door.

He pulls up the chair next to hers.

'Well, well. If it isn't my favourite author,' he teases. There's that insolent, crooked, dimpled smile again.

Rolling her eyes, she crosses her arms in front of her chest, as though trying to protect herself from his aggressive hotness. 'How much did you read?'

'Only till the part about their tongues doing a tribal dance in each other's mouths,' he says, grinning.

She groans, mortified, covering her face with a napkin.

'Oh, come on. You should be proud. I mean, I'd pegged you all wrong, kitten. Here I was thinking you're ... vanilla. But your books tell me a whole other story.' His tone still light and teasing, but the smile is gone and those grey eyes flare with an emotion she can't quite identify.

She blushes, while another part of her wonders why he's doing this – flirting with her when there are dozens of other hotter women around, wearing teeny-weeny bikinis. They'd all jump at the chance to be with him. She can see one hungrily checking him out right now.

She wonders if he has some kind of a fetish. Maybe this is his thing – unremarkable women in ugly oversized

T-shirts and basketball shorts, with messy hair and no makeup. Or maybe this is all an elaborate prank.

She eyes him suspiciously, asking, 'Where's your girlfriend?'

He looks confused for a moment, before he says, 'You mean ... Ana?'

She nods, sucking on her cigarette.

'We aren't dating, if that's what you were meaning to ask.'

That's definitely a part of what she was trying to do, but she would much rather feed herself to the wilkołak than admit it.

'Actually, I was asking because I have been meaning to speak to her. About Bliss,' she says.

His eyes narrow at that. 'What about it?'

She shrugs, 'I was reading up on the place last night and found some interesting insights.'

He doesn't seem to like the sound of that. 'And how does it concern you?'

'Research.'

He raises an eyebrow, 'On?'

She looks at the book in his hand, then back at him.

'Ah! The wilkołak? Is that what you were doing the night I found you?'

She nods.

'So, this murderer terrorizing North Goa – that's your next hero?' he asks with a laugh.

Tara doesn't take the bait. 'So will you introduce me to your girlfriend?' she counters instead.

'Be careful. You might just be stirring up a hornet's nest.' He sounds genuinely concerned.

'Come on, I just want a friendly chat!' she pleads.

He shakes his head, 'I'm afraid I can't put you in that position.'

'Fine,' she gets up, stubbing her cigarette and placing a two hundred-rupee note on the table. 'And thank you, for all your help,' she adds, her voice dripping with sarcasm.

His dimples reappear, as he shrugs, 'Maybe I'd be more helpful if we met somewhere nice for dinner? There's a cool Italian place right down the street.'

That does it! Tara sits back in her chair, placing her elbows on the table. She looks at him sternly, her tone business-like as she says, 'Why are you doing this?'

'What do you mean?'

'You know, asking me out on a date. Looking at me the way you are looking at me right now.' In response, his gaze – insolent and piercing – travels down her body and then back to her face. She feels tiny pinpricks of electricity everywhere it touches her.

His grin widens, as though he knows exactly the effect he has on her and takes pleasure in it. 'Am I not allowed to?'

'I mean, it's a free country,' she splutters. 'But just a heads-up, I'm not looking for a relationship.'

'Who said anything about a relationship, kitten?' That nickname sends a delicious shiver down her spine, while the rest of the words make her even angrier.

'What do you want then?' she demands.

A friend with benefits, perhaps? For a quick second, Tara imagines him leading her to that beach chair in the moonlight, and doing all the same things to her. She feels sweat drip down her back and cloud her upper lip, just at the thought of it.

A knowing smile plays on his lips, as though he can read her mind. 'Don't worry. I don't want that either,' he says.

A part of her is relieved, even as a small voice inside her whispers disappointedly, *Why?*

Reading her mind again, he replies, 'The thing is, Miss Tara Tandon, I have a feeling I'll make your werewolves look like puppies. Anyway, my intentions are entirely noble. A good dinner with some good company. That's all.'

'Fine, dinner it is,' she says, watching his expression turn cocky, victorious. 'But *after* the interview.'

'Touché! In the meantime, I look forward to finishing this,' he waves her book in the air. 'The characters definitely have *interesting* kissing techniques. Maybe I could learn a trick or two.'

She resists the urge to throw her coffee at him as she walks away.

'Do you dress up for all your interviews this sluttily?' Ahana teases from the phone screen. Her voice crackles and the video keeps freezing every couple of minutes, thanks to the terrible Wi-Fi.

Tara grimaces at her friend, before turning back to the mirror to apply her lipstick – a deep, matte red – and recheck her appearance for the hundredth time.

She's wearing a tight backless black dress with double spanx underneath. Though she can barely breathe, her cleavage has never looked better. Her hair is behaving, too, perhaps because she spent an hour straightening it into submission.

She looks around for her gold hoops frantically, as Ahana continues, 'Why do I feel like you're going on a date?'

'I'm noooooot!' Tara insists, blushing. 'I swear, it's all business. We're meeting Ana. Remember that chick I told you about? The one who may or may not be running a yoga cult in Morjim?'

'And what is it that you're hoping to find?'

'I dunno, I am going with an open mind.'

'So, is she on your list of potential werewolves?' While her best friend wasn't initially thrilled about Tara's new project, she seems to have come around in the past few days.

'I kinda hope she is? Can you imagine the feminist and homoerotic undertones? The toxic femininity of it all! Now, that's a book that critics will love,' Tara replies gleefully.

'I don't think that's what they meant—' Ahana says before the screen freezes again. Tara holds her phone up in the air for a bit, giving it a shake. She props it against the open window and Ahana's voice returns, '... and this guy? With the abs and dimples? You mean to say there's nothing there?'

'Well, I mean, he's hot,' Tara admits, before scrunching up her nose, 'But a little too hot, to be honest.'

'Tara—' Ahana says, before her voice starts to crack again, her face disintegrating into a thousand megapixels.

'Trust me, he's the last thing I need right now. I need to focus on the book. In fact, I solemnly swear to keep it in my pants,' Tara continues rambling, as she rummages around the suitcase in search of her elusive hoops.

'... right behind you,' Ahana says, her voice regaining its clarity, the pixels reassembling.

'What?' Tara asks, turning around to find Noel leaning against the doorway, grinning in amusement, dressed in an airy white shirt and blue jeans. But Tara has other, bigger concerns than how great he looks – like *how much of their conversation did he hear?!*

Still grinning, he walks past her and leans into the camera, waving at Ahana. 'Don't worry, I'll make sure your friend keeps it in her pants tonight,' he assures with a wink.

Tara groans, as she hangs up the call.

She's put way too much effort into her outfit tonight to overcompensate for her messy appearance this morning. Noel takes a good, slow look at her, his eyes darkening with a strange expression. His voice is particularly gruff as he says, 'You look hot ... a little too hot.'

Oh god, he heard it all.

He takes a step closer, and Tara's body reacts instantly. She looks into his smouldering eyes, and all but freezes as he leans towards her, lips hovering an inch above hers. His body is pinning her against the door behind her, and her heart beats loudly. She braces herself for what's coming next; closing her eyes, sucking in her breath ... until she hears a soft click. A blast of cold air hits her bare back.

'After you, ma'am,' he says with a smile. She sighs in relief, taking a second to gather her wits before leading him out.

They walk silently across the long, sandy stretch to the open-air jeep waiting at the beach exit. He drives a little too fast, his hands white-knuckled against the steering wheel. Tara spends the whole ride steadying her breath and trying to ignore the way the air between them crackles with electricity.

She's relieved when the car finally comes to a halt, taking a moment to smooth her rumpled dress and wind-whipped hair, all the while aware of his gaze fixed on her.

'Before we head inside,' he says, a playful glint in his eyes, 'we should probably pick a safe word.' The double entendre hangs in the air, adding to the tension.

'Ummm ... why?' she asks, frowning.

'Trust me, things could get gnarly in there.'

'I dunno. Crabs?' she offers.

He raises an eyebrow at her mood-killing choice of word. And she smiles back sweetly. 'What? I ate some last night and can't stop thinking about them.'

How's that for a double entendre?

He sighs. 'Crabs, it is.'

Placing a hand on her bare back, he leads her inside the modest two-storeyed red-brick building surrounded by a sprawling garden. Tara feels the effect of his touch in places that have nothing to do with her back.

A long hallway stretches into an open-air courtyard, with a dozen rooms on either side. The walls are covered with artworks depicting the naked female form in different styles, against myriad backdrops like forests, oceans and constellations. There are also some interesting oil paintings of animals surrounded by nature. A bear lounging with blue butterflies in a meadow, a crow in a black-and-white winter landscape, a panther in an enchanted Narnia-esque garden. Tara is drawn to one in particular – a wolf in a dark forest surrounded by vibrant wildflowers.

Around twenty women are seated in a circle in the courtyard, a fire roaring in the centre. Tara notices they are all predominantly white, and wearing flowing, white gowns. They regard their visitors with curious glances and those trademark creepy grins, but no one says a word until Ana enters the room.

There's something powerful about her presence. Her beauty is far from conventional: she's too pale, thin and tall, for starters. Her facial features are sharp and masculine, while her hair is slicked back, Tilda Swinton-style, all of which jars against the ultra-feminine settings. Her statuesque posture, haughty expression and booming voice command attention. It is clear why the rest of the women gravitate towards her. Ana looks like the kind of woman who has all the right answers, who might just understand the secrets of divinity and the universe.

'Come on in,' she says with a forced smile, her gaze resting longer than necessary on Noel's arm, still grazing Tara's back. 'We just finished our evening prayers.'

'These paintings are ... lovely,' Tara says. Her words seem to chip away at Ana's icy exterior.

'My art is inspired by nature, and all the wonderful women I meet,' she replies, gesturing at the ladies in the courtyard. 'This bear is Marianna,' Ana points to a middle-aged woman. 'She is strong but has a gentle soul. The crow is Olga, of course. Resilient, no matter how harsh life gets ...'

'And the wolf?' Tara asks.

Ana smiles. 'Ah! Noel told me you had particular fascination with ... the wilkołak?'

'I do, yes. Does the painting have something to do with it?'

Ana waves her off. 'Not at all. That's me. The duality of magic and madness, light and darkness, cosmic and earthly—'

'I see. But this wilkołak,' Tara presses on. 'Daria had mentioned it used to visit this place from time to time, that she had seen it.'

Ana sighs. 'Daria was troubled. Many months before her death, she said she was being visited by this wilkołak. She claimed she'd heard it clawing at her window. Pleading to be let inside. She felt like she was going mad.'

A shiver runs down Tara's spine, remembering her own similar experience two nights ago.

'Was it the same with ... Oksana?'

Ana nods. 'In my old village, the wilkołak was omen ... like Grim Reaper. It comes to you first in your dreams, then visions, then your doorstep, getting closer and closer until your time is up.'

Tara draws in a deep breath. *Is that what is happening to me, too?*

She tries to shove the disturbing thought away and asks Ana, 'So what do you think killed these women then, if not the wilkołak?'

Ana laughs, though her eyes remain humourless. 'Come on, we have much more dangerous enemies than wilkołak. It could have been any of them,' she shrugs.

'Who would be your top suspects, then?' Tara asks her, opening up the notes app on her phone. Ana shoots her an inscrutable look.

'You know, it's not easy for girls like Oksana and Daria. They were running from problems back home, and then they came here, only to find more of the same problems. You can hide from your past, from who you are – but it will always find you,' her eyes burn into Tara's as she says that, before she looks away, now addressing the wall behind her. 'These girls disappear all the time, and no one asks questions. The only reason they are talking now is because of these ... wilkołak rumours. No one really cares about *them*! That's why I started Bliss, to protect them.'

She shakes her head, a grave expression clouding her face as she looks at Tara again. 'Can I give you some advice?'

'Sure,' says Tara.

'Stop all this snooping around, because you won't like what you find. It's time for you to go home.'

'Is that a threat?'

'A threat? No, no, no.' She steps closer to Tara, holding her chin, making the latter flinch in response. 'I want to help you, *dorogaya*. You told me you saw the wolf that night, didn't you? That is a sign. You need to run.'

'But I saw it kill Daria.'

'Are you sure you can trust what your eyes saw that night? The liquid Daria gave you is very powerful. We drink it to reveal the secrets inside our heart. Maybe what you saw is what you wanted to see.'

'That doesn't make any sense.'

'Come, let me show you,' Ana smiles, taking Tara's hand and leading her to the courtyard. She motions her to sit on an empty cushioned stool right next to the fire.

'There's no need for that, Ana,' Noel interrupts, his voice loud and harsh. He grabs Tara's hand possessively, a flicker of warning in his eyes as he mouths the word 'crabs' to her.

'This is for her own good, Noel,' Ana insists, gently extricating Tara's hand from his grip.

'It's okay,' Tara tells him, with a small smile. 'I want to try it.'

Ana hands her a glass of the same foamy liquid she drank with Daria, as the women start praying in a language she doesn't understand. It sounds ancient, each word throaty and violent. They keep chanting for a long, long time, voices getting more and more ominous, until their eyes begin to glow yellow.

Tara gasps, turning to Ana, who opens her mouth, revealing a set of massive, razor-sharp canines and jagged molars. She lets out a deep, guttural growl.

7

Tara wakes up in a pitch-black room, before someone flips on the light switch. Fluorescent light assaults her vision. The space is a labyrinth of mirrors, each reflecting her insecurities – her round stubby nose, puffed up cheeks, uneven breasts, the cellulite dimpling her thighs, the folds in her back, the scars on her butt, until she can't bear it anymore.

In the distance, she can still feel a dozen pair of yellow eyes glare at her. She can hear them whisper disjointed words: 'Hack!', 'Talentless!' 'Mediocre!' 'Cancelled!' – until she's about to lose her mind. And then she disappears …

… replaced by a simple, singular heartbeat.

A nurse presses the ultrasound device over her mother's belly, rubbing it back and forth. She looks so … young, barely twenty-five, and her father still has a full head of hair. Tears of joy stream down their faces as they stare at the monitor. Like they've never seen anything more beautiful than this clump of cells ... this tiny flicker of life.

Everything feels so soft, snug and wet. Tara feels so safe and protected, she could stay here forever, but then she starts to twist and turn, feeling herself being squeezed and pushed out of her mother's body. She shoots down the narrow passage, the cold air hitting her with the force of a slap.

She lets out a loud angry wail.

'She's so beautiful, Nirmal,' she hears her mother say, choked with emotion. 'She's perfect,' he whispers back, his voice thick with tears.

Tara rises now, on her unsure, wobbly legs, making gurgling noises as she walks towards her mother's open arms. 'Ma – *ma*,' she manages to squeeze out the simple syllable to her parents' glee, and they bathe her in kisses. Their love so strong, so sure, so absolute, she feels more joy than her tiny heart could possibly hold.

The years start speeding by, and Tara watches a timelapse of herself growing, stretching, transforming, as she finally gains sentience. Standing before the mirror, she traces her features with her fingertips, fascinated by every detail. 'You have your mama's eyes,' her mother beams, her voice filled with pride. 'Don't forget my nose,' her father chimes in.

She feels a sickening lurch in her stomach as they start to fade into the sidelines.

She's in a park, surrounded by a group of sniggering teenagers. 'Fatty', they yell, making grunting, pig-like noises. Her face crumples, a delicate wire in her brain snapping. She looks in the mirror and all she can see is what they call her.

Everything is happening too fast now. First, come the breasts, then the belly, hair, blood and the bullies. She tries to stop it, rubbing her arms and legs vigorously with pumice stones and wearing her father's oversized T-shirts. She tries to miss breakfasts, then lunches and dinners, folding into herself, origami-ing her body into something delicate and swan-like, but she won't stop growing ...

'Oh, come on, it's cute!' the prettiest girl in school tells her in a baby voice, forcing Tara into a tiny dress from her wardrobe. Tara acts like she doesn't hear their laughter or the names they call her when she's not in the room. She downs too many shots of vodka that night, smokes too many cigarettes. 'What the hell, Tara!' the prettiest girl screams when Tara throws up all over her bed ...

'He likes you,' they tell her, pointing to the boy she feels nothing for. He's too old for her, his smile too leery. But they all act like he's doing her some kind of a favour. Who else will have her? 'Go on ...' they push her into a room with him. It all happens too quickly, before she can understand it. Before she can scream, 'I'm not ready!'

Something else snaps in her brain that night, too. She learns to become someone she is not. She learns to drift away and watch from the ceiling. She understands that her body is only an instrument to give pleasure, not take it. A sick part of her even revels in his desire for her ('*Who else will have you?*'), while another mourns her loss of innocence.

She can taste that familiar bitter feeling in her mouth now. *Self-hatred.*

'Stop!' She wants to scream. She can't relive the moment her parents found her sneaking back home, smelling the alcohol on her breath, whispering, 'You're too young for this, Tara'. She doesn't want to watch their faces crumple, as she screams, 'You don't get it!' Why are they so old-fashioned? So controlling? Why don't they understand that if she shaves every hair on her body, starves herself down to a certain number on the scale, wears the brightest lipstick, drinks the right amount of vodka and lets everybody have a piece of her dignity, she'll finally be worthy of something, of someone?

She watches her father's shoulders slump, her mother's eyes well up. They don't see her when they look at Tara, she realizes, all they see is that singular heartbeat. That miraculous clump of cells. *Their baby.*

The room spins ...

Now, she's in a forest like the one in Ana's painting, surrounded by wildflowers. She hears soft mewling noises in the distance. It's a puppy. It looks malnourished, and Tara can see the faint outline of its ribcage, the hunger in its eyes. 'Come here,' she whispers, watching it scamper towards her with something in its mouth. It drops it on the grass at her feet. It's her torn and tattered copy of *The Viking*. She remembers this cover so well ... a hulking man in an unbuttoned white shirt clutching a half-dressed woman in his arms. Her breasts spilling out of her bodice. Except, the Viking is now holding the chubby teenage Tara in his arms instead. The puppy runs off into the distance, bringing back more books – *The Bewitching Rake*, *The Philandering Count*, *The Reckless Viscount*, the Wild Nights with the Werewolf series ... She's on every cover, the object of the hero's adoring gaze.

When she finally looks back up, the puppy's already an adolescent. Awkward, scraggly, like that boy next door, whom she had a crush on for years. She offers it a plate of milk, and it takes a few hesitant sips before darting away. It comes back a few years later, leaner, with a mean glint in its eyes. She recognizes the small silver stud in its right ear. The same one her first boyfriend wore. She looks around and spots a rabbit. She kills and skins it, offering it to the mutt. She watches it lap the flesh up hungrily, before it slowly transforms into every man she has ever loved.

It disappears again. Tara waits patiently for its return, building herself a shelter with wood, decorating it with wildflowers. She guts every animal she encounters, skinning them, before drying out their entrails, and spicing and preserving their meat.

When the mutt returns, it looks different. Much larger than she had anticipated, though its coat is matted and covered in mange, revealing its gaunt frame underneath. Its eyes are hollow and sunken, and its head hangs low as it limps towards her. It devours all the meat she lays out, whimpering gratefully. Then, it places its head on her lap, headbutting her thigh, until she strokes it. Sighing, it wags its tail gratefully, curling into a ball by her feet, where it sleeps for weeks.

Slowly, she nurses the wounds on its body, feeding it with her own hands, watching proudly as its coat regains its shine, and its skeletal frame fills out with the arrival of rippling muscles. She watches it sprint through the forest, marvelling at its powerful strides.

Soon, it grows too big. The critters are no longer enough. It craves something more. She can hear its stomach rumble every time it looks at her.

Each time they play, it nips at her, which soon turns to nibbles. Sometimes, its slitted eyes shine with an expression so evil and ugly and familiar, it chills her blood.

It's the beast from her nightmares, she realizes. *Run,* a voice in her head says, *run before it's too late,* as she slowly watches it turn into a human figure she knows all too well.

Memories from a night long, long ago threaten to flood her brain. She can already taste that metallic flavour of her own blood in her mouth. Somewhere, far away, Tara can feel herself thrashing around, resisting what's coming after this.

'STOP. STOP THIS!' she hears herself scream.

'Don't fight it,' Ana's voice booms, drowning out her own. 'You need to confront your past.'

'ANA, STOP!' Noel thunders. 'Stop it right now!'

Then she feels Ana's hand on her own, as she says gently, 'Come back.'

With the help of her touch and voice, Tara slowly begins to register her surroundings. She lets go of Ana's hand, her cheeks burning with shame, as everyone stares at her in silence.

'Let's go,' Noel says, wrapping an arm around Tara, before turning to Ana in anger, 'Why do you always have to take it so far?'

'I was trying to help. She can handle it!' Ana cries out as he leads Tara away.

He drives in silence. His hand finds hers somewhere along the way, and he doesn't let go till he drops her to her room.

'I am so sorry,' Noel says gently. 'I shouldn't have let her do this to you.'

Tara still isn't quite sure what happened. All she knows is that she needs to be alone.

'I don't think we should see each other for a while,' she tells him.

He looks like she's just slapped him in the face.

'I don't think I am in the right frame of mind,' she tries to explain. 'Being around you makes me feel things I am not prepared for. I'm afraid you and I ... whatever this is ... it's not a good idea. At least not right now.'

He sighs, running a hand through his hair. 'Alright, kitten. If that's what you want.'

She puts her ear to the door, waiting till the sound of his footsteps fade. Then, the dam breaks. Her sobs turn into loud, awful howls, ripping from her gut.

When she's done, she goes out to the balcony and lights a cigarette, staring at the sea.

Her stomach flips when she spots it – the massive shape in the distance, all but blending into the night, save for its yellow glowing eyes. It seems to be leaning its body weight against its hind legs; almost *puppy-like*, as though inviting her to play. It runs around in circles before throwing its head back and letting out a howl that mirrors hers before bounding away.

8

In the days that follow, Tara spends most of her time searching for new leads on Ana. Sunny begrudgingly continues to help her, taking her to the beaches around North Goa and helping her find new sources. They analyze their findings for hours at Shakti Shack. Sunny insists he is doing all this because she 'lacks self-preservation instincts' (he still can't believe she *willingly* let the women at Bliss drug her again). But Tara knows better. Sunny is softening towards her. Maybe even becoming a friend.

While the jury is still out on whether a wilkołak exists, she's sure Ana had something to do with those murders. Tara visits the night market for two consecutive Saturdays, even learning broken Russian phrases to converse with the expats settled in Arambol, Morjim and Mandrem.

Meanwhile, Noel stands by his word. She doesn't hear from him.

She hasn't been visited by the beast either, be it in her beach hut or her dreams. Perhaps because all her waking thoughts are consumed by her research. It takes a while to make any headway. Ana's name often seems to evoke an uneasy silence. Most of the times, Tara is sent away with dirty looks.

Ana must have become aware Tara was poking around, because days ago, she had sent her a little gift, wrapped in brown paper. She had torn it open to find one of her oil paintings. A short, stocky creature with a black-and-white striped face and tiny legs, in a forest bathed in blue moonlight. Tara had scoffed in disbelief at the passive-aggressive note that accompanied it:

> Dearest Tara,
>
> The honey badger is the most underrated prey in the forest, not only because it's stubborn, relentless and thick-skinned, but also because it packs a surprising ferociousness and fearlessness underneath. It doesn't just survive venomous snake bites, bee stings and attacks from predators thrice its size, it bites back.

A fucking honey badger? Not sure whether to see the 'gift' as an insult or a compliment, Tara had stuffed the painting to the bottom of her suitcase, carrying on with her investigation until she found an unlikely source in a DJ at a local club, who had helped an ex-member, Sasha, escape from Bliss.

'It wasn't easy to leave. In fact, it's one of the hardest things I have ever done,' Sasha, who is back in Russia, tells her over the phone. 'It's not like we were handcuffed or tied up, at least not physically. But once you're in, it's almost like you're bound to Bliss and Ana. She knows how to get inside your head, find your biggest fears and insecurities, and use them to control you.

'The first time we met, she instantly recognized what I was lacking in my life: meaning. Ever since my parents died in a sudden car crash, I'd been wandering around the world using whatever savings I had. After backpacking across Europe and Asia, I was running out of both money and ideas about where to go next. In Goa, I came across an old friend from back home who was a member of Bliss. She spoke about how Ana had recently helped her escape an abusive relationship, and the other women she was supporting. She made them all sound like one big, happy family. When she was done talking, I practically begged her to take me to the Bliss quarters!'

There's a short pause before Sasha continues, 'That first night was wonderful. They all welcomed me with open arms and plenty of food – dishes like borscht, pirozhki and khychin that reminded me of home. I could see how much all these women loved each other. It was obvious from the constant chatter and the laughter.

They worked together in coordination while cooking, serving and cleaning. It was like watching a beautiful dance on stage. And Ana ... oh, how she fascinated me! I could see why they called her "mother". She reminded me so much of my own. Like a coconut, they were both hard on the outside, yet soft inside. But to get to the soft part, you had to prove yourself worthy of their love and approval. I was lucky. That first night, I could tell that Ana already saw something in me. She stayed by my side, asking me many questions about my life, as if I was the most interesting person she had ever met. Maybe that's why I fell under her spell immediately.

'It felt strange, but also good. Being among all these people made me realize just how lonely and homesick I was. Ana could see it, too. She invited me to stay back, said she was looking for someone with administrative experience, who could speak fluent English while dealing with the locals there. I felt honoured that she wanted me beside her. For the first time in ages, I felt like I had a purpose – helping women and making a real difference. I was a part of something bigger than myself. But it all began to fall apart very quickly.

'The deeper my involvement with Bliss became, the more I realized that Ana was helping no one but herself. Most of the women there came to her during troubled times. When they had no one else to turn to. No family, friends or money. Often battling addiction or dealing with trauma and abuse. They were broken and vulnerable and once Ana "helped" them, they felt indebted to her. That's when the brainwashing would start.

'At first, you don't even realize you're losing your free will. That someone is telling you what to wear, how to behave, whom to talk to. Our routine, our jobs, our beliefs – everything was decided for us. I gave all my remaining money to Bliss, leaving everyone in the outside world behind. The psychedelic she regularly gave us, Psilocybin, made us all the more vulnerable. It broke down every wall and left us completely at her mercy. The experience was like what they call a complete "ego death". It's like you don't remember who you are. You're outside your body. It can feel spiritual. It can feel like enlightenment or meeting God. It made us feel like we were all connected, that the universe had somehow conspired to bring us together. The one thing we all had in common was that we were starving for love. And that's what Bliss gave us, at least at first – instant acceptance and sisterhood. What we didn't understand was that the sisterhood was an illusion. That we were all being skilfully manipulated by Ana; socially, psychologically, financially, spiritually ...

'It was only much later that I realized this "magical bond" tying us all together was a ruthless bureaucratic system keeping us in check. We were always afraid to say or do the wrong thing, lest we appear ungrateful or rebellious. It's like you were always being watched and judged. The slightest misstep and you would be reported to Ana. The punishment was isolation and shunning. The whole idea was to cut down any individuality. You were kept trapped in this cycle of guilt, shame and fear.'

'Sounds a lot like an abusive relationship,' Tara says.

'It was! Once you were in too deep, having given all your money and agency to Ana, the pressure grew. Unknowingly, you were pushed down a path you didn't want. Helping her grow and sell drugs. Sleeping with powerful men in return for favours. "Do it for the family," they'd say, making it sound altruistic, as though you'd be selfish if you didn't. Ana was never forceful; she would always sound so logical. As if it were a choice, even though there was none. Part of a higher plan, a rung in our spiritual ladder.

'Soon, I started protesting, asking questions. The others warned me to leave it be. To keep my head down and do whatever Ana said for my own good. But I just couldn't. I wanted to leave many times. Almost did once or twice, but I would always chicken out. After all, this was my family. It was the only life I knew. Besides, I had no money and no idea where I would go.'

'What made you finally leave?'

'It was when my friend, the one who introduced me to Bliss, killed herself. She had been struggling with

PTSD, and Bliss made it worse. They discouraged her from seeking help. In fact, Ana insisted that she was the only one who could heal her. That finally opened my eyes. I knew that I could never forgive Ana and wouldn't be able to live with myself if I stayed.'

'Were you ever afraid that Ana would ... hurt you for leaving? Do you think that's something she's capable of doing?'

'I was terrified for years. I think she's very capable of hurting someone for doing what I did. Especially if that someone has seen or heard too many things.'

Two days later, Tara's sitting in the balcony with her notes, when she sees Noel.

He looks good, shirtless as usual, playing volleyball on the beach. There's a brunette in a skimpy red bikini getting incredibly handsy with him, and he doesn't seem to mind. When they're done with the game, she watches them disappear together in the waves for a bit, laughing and splashing water at each other, like they're in some rom-com.

Tara's face tightens as she burns with red-hot jealousy and pure, white rage. She knows her reaction is ridiculous – wasn't she the one to end things with him?

Still, he could have taken a minute to mourn whatever we had, she whines internally.

And what is it that you 'had', Tara? You didn't even kiss him. Stop acting like a fool!

She continues staring at him resentfully. It's hard to take her eyes off him. The man is pure muscle and she's hypnotized by the way his body bunches and relaxes with each movement.

Her gaze travels up to his face that's just as chiselled as the rest of him, as though carved in stone. It's like staring at Michelangelo's David, except that he wouldn't stare back at her like Noel is doing right now, she realizes.

Fuck.

As soon as their eyes lock, Tara begins squirming in her chair. Those grey eyes. It's been a while since she's had them on her, and she instantly finds herself breathless and agitated.

She watches him whisper something to the woman, then walk out of water, heading straight for her.

Oh no. She's not ready to face him, not yet. She watches in horror as he keeps walking, pausing to grab his towel from a beach chair. His eyes never leave hers. When he's finally beneath her balcony, he shakes the water out of his hair and wipes his body down before draping the towel around his broad shoulders.

'What's up, kitten?' he calls out from below. 'Playing the Peeping Tom again?'

'I was just watching the sunset!' she cries in return. 'It's not my fault you're right there.'

He flashes her a mischievous smile, his dimples making her stomach twist.

She opens her mouth to say something, anything, but her brain has stopped working. They stay there, silent, eyes locked in a gaze that feels thrilling and illicit.

Then the brunette sneaks up behind him, grabbing his waist. He bends down, letting her climb on his back.

Tara feels like she's been doused with a bucket of cold water.

He smiles at her as he waves goodbye. 'See you around, I guess.'

She glares at him before stomping back inside.

That does it. Tara needs to Marie Kondo him out of her mind and her life. She needs a change of scenery.

9

Sunny is sitting across from her at the burger joint in Anjuna, wearing a breezy cotton shirt, khakis, loafers and a confused look on his face. The moustache – that had her screaming 'nerd alert!' the first time she met him – kind of suits him, she realizes.

She's wearing a halter-neck dress, with psychedelic spirals all over it, and her favourite bright red lipstick, but he doesn't seem to notice or care how she looks.

'So, let me get this clear, this is not about the case?' he asks for the tenth time.

'I just wanted to hang out,' Tara says, between huge bites of her burger. 'You know, we've never really hung out.'

He looks even more befuddled at that.

'Go on, tell me more about yourself,' Tara asks with a bright smile. 'How did you become a cop?'

'I gave the exam and passed,' he says impatiently.

Tara sighs, switching to thc only topic he's comfortable with. 'So what's the latest in Daria's case?'

'Nothing yet,' he shakes his head. 'They still seem to be looking for this elusive animal. Between you and me, this one's never going to be solved.'

He politely offers to drop her home after she demolishes her burger and drains three glasses of wine.

'What? We're going home? No, not yet!' she whines.

He looks confused over her desire to prolong the night.

'Come on. The night's too young. Let's go dancing!' she says, yanking his arm, feeling loose-limbed and adventurous.

'I don't dance,' he shakes his head.

'Let's go to Club Coyote!' she squeals, as they make their way to his scooty. She knows she's about to make a huge mistake, but she's too drunk to care.

'I hate that place,' Sunny groans.

'Fine, then. I'll go there alone, I guess,' she says grumpily.

They stare at each other in silent anger for a few seconds, before Sunny sighs. 'Just get on the damn bike. An hour tops, then we are leaving!'

They arrive at the foot of the cliff where Coyote stands, shooting streaks of lasers into the sky. As they park, she spots a large group of bouncers with walkie-talkies, ushering guests into a jeep that carries them up a hill. It feels like they are headed to a deliciously illicit operation. A war zone? Blood diamond mines? Who knows.

It builds up a weird anticipation inside Tara, as she is packed in the vehicle along with Sunny and three bald white men, who sound Swedish from the rhythm of their indecipherable conversation.

When they get off at the top floor, it's pitch dark save for phosphorous columns leading to the dance floor, where a tent made up of fluorescent greens and pinks and blues billows like a translucent psychedelic jellyfish in the sky. The crowd is moving like one sweaty entity to music that isn't even music – just ear-splitting beats overlapping with extraterrestrial noises that get her heart pumping, nonetheless.

Women in tight, barely-there corsets and skirts walk around with trays of flaming shots, while others dance in cages, waving around their hot pink-feathered tails and headdresses.

Tara looks up to see there's another level to the club, with glowing, posh-seeming cabanas, the people inside roped off and heavily guarded like they're royalty.

She feels her heart start to race as she spots who she had been expecting (and hoping) to see in the biggest private enclosure. Even while seated, he towers over everyone else, in his white linen shirt and pyjamas that are fluttering in the wind. There's a woman draped across his lap, the brunette from the beach. He doesn't seem all that interested in her, though. She watches the woman whisper and giggle in his ear, but even though one of his hands is tracing her thigh absent-mindedly, the other is scrolling through his phone.

He looks bored out of his mind.

Good, Tara thinks, then feels a surge of self-hatred. She tries to repent by focusing on Sunny again. He's standing there in the most police-like stance possible. His arms crossed, his feet spread apart, a threatening look on his face like he's about to tell someone, 'You're under arrest.'

'Let's do shots!' she says to him. But as they plonk themselves on the bar-stools, Sunny launches into a long rant about how this place needs to be shut down. 'Everything's so overpriced,' he complains. 'The bugger's a thief.'

Thankfully, she can barely hear him over the beats.

As he drones on and on about what they found here during the last drug raid, she looks at him with a glazed expression, letting her inner monologue take over.

What's wrong with you, Tara?

Why can't you get over that ass? He took less than five minutes to move on from you!

You should see a therapist, you know.

No, don't look at that cabana! Look away from that man, right now, *Tara Tandon!*

But she can't stop herself from staring at Noel every few seconds. After shot number two, she's approached by one of the all-black-wearing, walkie-talkie-carrying bouncers.

'Boss wants you to join them in the VVIP box,' he says to her, motioning to the cabana she's been staring at all evening.

'Tell him no, thanks,' Sunny shuts the bouncer down.

'Come on!' Tara groans, grabbing his hand. 'Let's at least *try* to have some fun.'

The bouncer escorts them up the stairs, past two security checkpoints.

Despite pretty much summoning her to his enclosure, Noel seems distracted when they arrive and take the seat across from him. Turns out, after ignoring the brunette all evening, Noel has suddenly found that he is indeed interested in her, after all. In fact, he is so fascinated with whatever his date seems to be saying to him that he doesn't even look at Tara.

Tara puts on an equally impressive display of her own acting skills by feigning nonchalance at the way his hands and eyes are roaming over the brunette's body. She barely even breaks character when he bends down to kiss the woman, while she and Sunny sit there like some kind of sideshow.

Of all the twisted power games.

He's a terrible nightclub host.

Shaking her head, she pulls out a cigarette from her clutch and walks away from the cabana to the edge of the floor. One of the bouncers sprints to her enthusiastically to light it. She puffs on it and watches the jellyfish tent expand and contract below, as the crowd gets more frantic. She feels a similar, strange build-up in her belly, a churning of emotions she can't quite place a finger on.

Two can play this game, she thinks.

'See, I told you we shouldn't have come here. I can't watch any more of their tonsil hockey,' Sunny is grumbling beside her now, but she barely even registers him. The night's turned into a big *Queen's Gambit* chess board above her head, and all she sees standing next to her is a tall, lanky, moustachioed pawn.

'Who cares?' she shrugs, grabbing his shirt and pulling him closer, bringing her lips to his. The kiss is mechanical, and it feels like ... *nothing* – perhaps because Tara's anger is acting like a bit of an anaesthesia. She breaks away to look at Noel after a sufficient amount of time has passed. He seems to have finally disentangled himself from the woman and is looking at her with an inscrutable expression. One she finds that she quite enjoys. She wants to swirl and sip it in a wine glass. *I detect some notes of anger? The tartness of jealousy?*

Tara raises her brow at him. *Your move.*

When they're back in their seats in the cabana, Noel's the very picture of cool, calm and composed again. He's lounging in his seat, his date relegated again to the sidelines. 'I'm sorry ... we were a bit caught up,' he says, as he hands each of them pink shots. Tara barely recognizes his tone – distant and polite. He's acting like he barely knows her.

'Never mind. Sunny's showing me around Goa, and we thought we'd check this place out,' Tara smiles, trying to match his distantly polite tone, as she picks up another shot.

She's about to knock it back when his eyes meet hers and she almost sees a familiar, mischievous glint in them.

'So do you like it?' he asks, a bit too cockily.

'It's nice – quite big and all. A bit tacky, though. All those girls dancing in cages like exotic birds. It makes me sad.'

'Don't be. We let them out from time to time,' Noel says, straight-faced, though she sees a hint of a dimple.

Then he turns his attention to her companion. 'So, Sunny! When did you start playing on *this* team?' he says, motioning to Tara with his chin.

Tara narrows her eyes. 'What do you mean?'

'He used to be gay,' Noel shrugs.

'Still am,' Sunny says, sheepishly.

'Why didn't you tell me?' Tara cries, turning a bright shade of red.

'How could I, with your tongue in my mouth like that!' he shoots back.

Tara catches a glimpse of the smug grin on Noel's face, and resists the urge to bury her face in her hands. Instead, she shoots him a withering look, as she tries to muster the last of her dignity. 'I'm going to dance!' she declares.

Sunny starts whining again. 'It's way past midnight already.'

She ignores him and heads down. She can feel Noel's eyes follow her all the way to the dance floor. She feels them on her as she starts moving to the beats. She sees a tall, blond man looking at her, and she flashes him a smile. He joins her in a flash.

Unfortunately for her, he is not much of a dancer. He throws his arms and legs around in moves that have zero correlation to the music, almost punching her in the stomach and taking her eye out at one point. She's stopped dancing now and is more concerned with dodging his next hit. She's also feeling painfully aware of the fact that Noel is watching her make a fool of herself from the skies.

A bit deflated at the thought of having lost their silly mind game, she excuses herself to head towards the bar, where she starts pounding shots, hoping the bitterness of the vodka will cancel out the bitterness and confusion inside her.

Shot one. *What was she thinking going up against a seasoned player like him?*

Shot two. *She's no match!*

Shot three. *She's just a stupid girl who—*

A warm, steady pair of hands grab her waist. She doesn't even have to turn around to know who they belong to. She could recognize them, and his scent, anywhere.

Without turning her around, Noel brings her closer to him, lifting her up till her feet are on his. Their hips move together seamlessly. Like they know this dance, like they've been doing it for years. He's moving against her in a rhythm that feels forbidden, like they are already in his bed. She feels his warm lips nuzzle her neck, and a tiny moan slips out.

He hears it, and finally spins her around to face him; his hands possessive on her hips, their bodies melded together. Despite the fact that she's matching his every move – her hands all over him, too – she stares at his Adam's apple because she can't bring herself to look him in the eye. She feels his fingers travel from her hips to her side, slowly tracing and caressing their way to her neck, till he lifts her chin, forcing her to look into his darkened eyes.

His hips continue to move against hers in a slow, hot and deliberate manner. He wants her just as bad. She can see it in his eyes.

Finally, his gaze releases her, as he bends down to let his lips trace her neck again. He nips her skin – just a small bite, really – and whispers, 'Turns out, I like the taste of vanilla.'

They break apart when the song ends, and Tara realizes he's left her dress and hair completely dishevelled and her heart rate out of control. As she calms down, running her hands through her curls to tame them, she sees both Sunny and the brunette standing there, looking confused, disappointed and a bit mad.

'Guess we just lost our dates, eh?' Noel grins besides her, not looking the least bit apologetic.

They're in his SUV, on the way back to her hotel. Dark, deserted roads unfurl before them, beckoning them to stop the car, and finish whatever they had started on the dance floor. Tara feels uncomfortable, squirming in the seat next to him, even though she still can't look at him. She feels hotboxed by their silence and chemistry.

She focuses on his hands gripping the steering wheel unnaturally hard. She stares at them longingly, while realizing that she's sexually objectifying his arm – tattooed, strong, veiny, with sprinkles of dark hair ... wow, now she's turning it into some sort of a phallic symbol, like she's in a Charlotte Brontë novel or something. His other hand reaches to push back his hair, and Tara doesn't know why that simple act drives her crazy. She wants those hands on her. Now.

Her stomach churns with all the shots from before, and the strange anticipation that he'll stop the car any second now …

He doesn't.

Instead, he drives her straight to her doorstep. She fiddles endlessly with the lock on the front door in the hopes of him making a move. He just stands next to her with his hands in his pockets, like he has zero intentions of doing anything of the sort.

Like nothing happened.

She gives the lock another half-hearted jiggle, hoping Noel will do something, *anything*. But now he's looking around distractedly, as though wishing she'd hurry up so he can go home.

She hates the power he has over her. Finally, and to his apparent amusement, she almost breaks the lock open in frustration, and pushes the door with unnecessary force to step inside. She's about to slam it in his grinning face, when she makes a last-ditch attempt.

'Do you want to … come in?' she whimpers, feeling disgusted with her desperation.

'Why?' he asks with a raised eyebrow, feigning confusion, except she can see right through his silly facade. He is goading her, reducing her to begging like this.

'To finish what we …' she clears her throat, 'started.'

He steps forward, his lips hovering close to hers as he whispers, 'What did we start?'

'Nothing,' she chokes out, feeling ridiculed. *Maybe he is right. What did we even start?*

Just as she's about to accept defeat, that smile – teasing, taunting – returns. He traces a finger down her cheek, then her neck, stopping at the delicate spot above her breasts. Tara is sure he can feel her heart jumping under his hand, because the damn thing is pounding in her ears. Before she can catch her breath, she feels his other hand grab her waist in a possessive grip as he brings his lips down to hers.

10

Tara wakes up with messy hair, bruised lips and their searing kiss playing on loop in her mind. A kiss that had lasted till the wee hours. She keeps going back and pressing play at the moment he grabbed her and pinned her against the door. Pausing at the moment his lips clamped down hungrily on her, his tongue finding her own. Fast forwarding to when they were in bed, his hand slipping under her dress.

She remembers his ragged breaths as he had said, 'We have to stop ...' while she whispered back frantically, 'No, no, we really don't.' Her hands were already fumbling with the buttons of his shirt.

The way he had held them back gently, kissing each fingertip. 'I thought you wanted to take things slow.'

That storm in his eyes as she had replied, 'Yeah, well, fuck slow.'

'No, kitten. I want to do this the right way. Let's start with that dinner date you promised me.'

And then with a last flash of his dimples, he was gone.

'Ugh,' she says out loud, before replaying the whole sequence of events again. Eventually, in a desperate bid to release all the pent-up sexual frustration, Tara decides to go for a jog. She puts on a pink sports bra with matching spandex tights, and laces up her shoes.

A sudden shock of rain has turned the beach into a Gogh-ish landscape. The sky and ocean look like they have been painted with thick, haphazard brush strokes of varying blues and greys, the sand's a mix of deep wet browns and dry yellows. There's that earthy smell in the air as Tara begins her slow jog.

And there he is.

Tara can't help but smile as she spots Noel's big hulking back. God, she can already feel herself getting tingly. He is sitting on a boulder facing the ocean that's swollen from the rain, the waves threatening to wash him away.

'That looks dangerous,' she calls out.

He turns, and for a moment, she feels disoriented by what she's looking at – it's Noel's face, but it's all wrong. Like someone has rearranged his features ever so slightly, and then disfigured them with a gnarly scar across the entire left half.

She gasps audibly, and somewhat rudely. He flinches, as though used to people reacting to him in this manner.

'I am sorry, I thought you were someone I know,' she tries to cover her misstep and not focus too much on that massive scar.

From the bitter smirk on his face, she can tell he sees right through her. 'I am guessing you mean my brother, Noel.'

She nods, noticing again how similar they are – down to the length of their hair, the dimples and the crooked smile. He's a little shorter and stockier than Noel, though, and a decade younger. He's also dressed differently, in a sweatshirt and loose shorts.

'I didn't know he had a brother,' she says.

'You're his new ... plaything, I suppose?' he asks, inching closer. His gait is a bit wobbly, and she notices the beer bottle in his hand.

'Wow, way to be respectful, dude,' she huffs, taking a few steps back. He's too close for comfort now. So close that she can see that his right eye is the same shade as his brother's, but there's something off about the other one. It's a different colour and remains frozen in its socket.

The smile on his face softens as he registers her words. 'Yeah, that was rude. I guess we're even now.'

'I'm sorry for staring,' she says. 'You're so *alike*.'

The smile's gone as he almost spits out the words at her, 'Nah, I am nothing like him.'

The vitriol in his voice makes her back away. 'Right,

anyway, please carry on,' she rambles, pointing to his beer.

As she resumes her run, she hears him call out, 'Don't waste your time on him! Goa has a lot more to offer than that piece of shit.'

She shoots him an awkward thumbs-up sign as she runs away as fast as she can.

She doesn't know what to make of this encounter, suddenly realizing just how little she knows of Noel.

And yet here she is, halfway in love with him.

'I don't understand it,' Vik says, later at night, as he goes through Tara's new draft. 'First, there's your disjointed rambling about being eaten by a beast. Second, this werewolf case, which feels ridiculous! Then, there's the cult stuff. I mean, it's all meaningless hotch-potch at this point.'

'Well, it's not *done* yet,' Tara says defensively, seated by the window where her Wi-Fi signal is strongest. Not strong enough, though, since the video continues to freeze and lag. 'But I just know there's a common thread tying it all together.'

Vik's face freezes in a disapproving look. She gets a pillow to shove under her laptop to unfreeze him.

'Finally!' he calls out. 'Look, I have to be honest with you. Things are not looking good here. Rhino is having second thoughts. Do you know there's a BoycottTara hashtag on Twitter now? I mean, there's only a handful of such tweets, but still ...'

'This is getting ridiculous,' Tara splutters. 'But I really think this book is going to fix everything.'

Vik sighs. 'I just think you have this talent for romance books—'

'Weren't you the one who said that all I do is write smut?' she narrows her eyes at him.

'Which takes talent, Tara! Just because you make it look easy, doesn't mean it is easy. You know exactly what all those women want, what gets them wet and worked up ...'

Tara shoots him a disgusted look.

'You're the "last bastion of female fantasy", remember?' he throws her words back in her face. 'All you have to do is tweak the formula just a bit to pacify the woke mob.'

She shakes her head this time, before pausing to collect her thoughts in a way that makes Vik double-check if she's still there.

'I just don't think I'm in the headspace – I mean, maybe the woke mob was right all along. Maybe I need to heal and confront my demons. Maybe my books are more damaging than I once thought,' she rambles on before she notices that his face is no longer in the Zoom window.

All she sees on the screen is an elaborate ergonomic empty chair against a shelf with book titles arranged pleasingly in order by colour. His desk is a little too neat, stacked with manuscripts, little plants and expensive-looking candles.

She waits for him to return, focusing on her miniscule self in the tiny Zoom window at the bottom of the screen instead. Her hair is sticking out at various angles, and she seriously can't remember the last time she brushed it. Her eyebrows haven't been threaded since she came to Goa and they look like two caterpillars edging towards each other, desperate to mate.

Her eyes spy some movement behind her, and her heartbeat quickens. She sees it lurking right outside the window, its yellow eyes hovering above her face, the rest of it camouflaged against the dark night.

'Vik!' she whispers, as the creature growls over her shoulder.

He walks back to his laptop, wiping his hands with a towel, rambling about his slow-cooked pulled chicken almost being done, when she snaps at him again, 'Do you see it?'

Between several stop motion-like starts and pauses, she watches Vik finally squint at the Zoom window and register what's behind her.

'What the fuck, Tara! You need to close that window! Not the Zoom video, you idiot. The window behind you!'

She turns around to find herself face to face with the beast – and it's really a creature from some other world. Time stands still, as everything around her fades. She feels like she's on drugs again, because this thing just can't be real.

Its face is three times the size of hers and so close that she can see the fine hairs of its coal black fur, her own reflection in its yellow eyes, as it sniffs and studies her. It's so close that she can feel its warm acrid animal breath on her face.

It's grinning at her, the same way it had the night it murdered Daria – a smile that's both dangerous yet leery. She notices how its ears are pulled back, as it emits a low guttural growl, its yellow fangs stained with blood.

'What are you doing, Tara? Get away! It's about to attack you!' she hears Vik scream in the distance.

But right when it's about to sink those massive fangs into her, it retreats back into the shadows.

Its growls intermingle with the sound of the howling wind outside, before fading away.

Trembling, Tara shuts the window, but not before she spots the moon in the sky – full and bright.

'You have to leave,' Sunny begs. 'This is too dangerous. That thing could kill you.'

She had phoned him after Noel refused to answer any of her calls. Sunny had arrived along with a friend from the Forest Department to check what had attacked Tara, but the creature was long gone. The rain had wiped away the pugmarks, too.

Leave.

Go home.

Run before you get hurt.

She has been given the same advice a million times by a million people, and yet Tara can't find it in herself to take it. Not until she's done.

'That's the thing, Sunny. It could have killed me so easily. It's almost like it didn't want to,' she tells him, realizing just how ridiculous and deranged the words sound.

Even if it did, you wouldn't let that stop you now, right, Tara? the beast in her head taunts her. *You're not going to let the haters win. Oh no, you're going to prove you're a 'great writer' even if it kills you!* The beast laughs. *Oh, Tara. This has always been your pattern, hasn't it? You just never know when to stop.*

She's always flown too damn close to the sun. Till she could literally feel her wings melt, till she was hurtling to the ground, the only choice left to crash and burn.

Till she was stuck in a hospital, listening to a doctor describe what had happened to her in terms she didn't entirely understand. 'What you have is an anterior globe laceration, Tara.'

She recalls that awful night. All the blood. *Her* blood.

She'd ignored all the warning signs then, too. Chased after danger like a fool with a death wish.

'You can hide from your past, from who you are,' Ana had said, 'but it will always find you.'

And oh, was she right!

The thing is, there is this ugly side of Tara. Pathetic, needy, sneaky. One that will stop at nothing, go to every length to prove that she is worthy ... of love, validation, approval, acceptance. This side of her – with a bottomless hunger, an insatiable need to be 'enough' for someone – is more dangerous and destructive than she'd like. It is an addict, twitching for its next hit – a sly, stealthy liar with zero conscience, who'd steal the clothes off your back to get what it wants.

It takes things too far. It never realizes when it is time to leave, to fucking *let go*.

Tara rushes to the bathroom, splashing cold water on her face. Then, she looks up in the mirror.

She notices the purple crescents under her eyes, which have a haunted look in them.

She's seen that look before.

It's the same one she saw in Oksana and Daria's eyes before they died.

11

'Cult Leader Found Dead in Morjim Home'.

Tara stares at the headline, a chill running down her spine. Underneath it is a picture of Ana standing alongside her followers, all wearing the same flowing white robes and unsettlingly wide smiles.

She was found naked, her body riddled with silver bullets. The word '*chudovische*', which translated to 'monster' in English, was scrawled upon her back using her own blood. It happened while the rest of the group was participating in one of their full moon ceremonies on Morjim beach, right behind the house.

According to the article, one of Ana's followers, Marianna Stolyarov, has admitted to killing her in self-defence. 'I saw her turn into the wilkołak right before my eyes,' she's quoted as saying. 'Ana's the one who killed my sisters Daria Chernova and Oksana Petrova.'

However, the report added that there is no evidence to substantiate Marianna's claims about Ana.

'Toxicology reports also indicate the presence of a high dose of Psilocybin in Marianna's system at the time of the murder. While the authorities have remained tight-lipped about the case so far, sources say Goa Police also uncovered a Psilocybin mushroom plantation at the house. Ana's followers are reportedly being investigated for their involvement in drug trafficking as well as their legal status, since many of their visas were found expired.'

Tara struggles to wrap her head around the news as she speaks to Sunny over the phone. 'So I was right? Ana really was a werewolf?'

'Well, there is zero evidence to suggest that,' he says. 'And since Marianna isn't a credible enough witness, I guess we'll never really know.'

'I am a witness too, though! I saw the creature hours before the murder – and I was fully sober this time, too!' she cries.

'It's not enough, Tara,' he says.

She sighs. 'Why does this feel like square one?'

She hangs up and trudges resentfully through the sand to her hut.

Noel's waiting for her at the stoop of the hut. She tries to avoid him by heading in the other direction, but he grabs her arm, forcing her to look into his eyes – bloodshot, with dark shadows underneath. He looks like he hasn't slept all night.

'I'm sorry I missed your calls yesterday. It was so busy at the club, and then I heard about Ana,' he says now, his voice hoarse with emotion.

Tara had sworn to never forgive him but the anger melts as she looks into his tortured eyes.

'It's okay,' she tells him. 'I am so sorry about Ana.'

He gives her a small smile, as he pulls her down into his lap. She weaves her fingers through his. They remain there in silence for a long time.

Finally, he says, 'Ana and I ... our relationship was complicated. I didn't always agree with her. God knows I couldn't stand her sometimes. We'd go months without speaking. Still, she was family. The only one I had.'

The statement strikes Tara as weirdly incestuous. Also, hadn't she met his brother the day before? But she doesn't say that out loud, since he's obviously in mourning.

'The things they are calling her ... a cult leader. A werewolf,' Tara begins.

Noel shakes his head in disgust. 'Ana was no saint. Sure, she was involved in all sorts of illegal things. But these women, they had nowhere to go. Ana gave them a roof over their head and a livelihood. You can disagree with her style of doing it, but you have to admit that she was the only one in these women's corner. She was all they had. I don't know what's going to happen to them now.'

Tara nods, biting her lower lip, remembering all the things Sasha had said about how controlling and abusive Ana was, and how she took advantage of the women. But she isn't sure she wants to argue over Ana with Noel right now; not while he's in this state.

'Was it important?' he asks.

She looks at him in confusion.

'The reason you were calling me last night?'

She tells him about her encounter with the wolfish creature the night before, and she can feel his body tense under hers. 'I should have been there. I should have protected you,' he says, guilt and shame flickering across his face, as he grips her tighter.

'It's really not that big of a deal. See? I am totally unscathed,' she smiles brightly.

He looks at the beach hut, and then back at her. 'You can't stay in this hovel any longer, Tara,' he says.

'The thing is, I'm kinda broke and—' she begins.

'Come home with me,' he cuts her off.

'No, I don't want to burden you,' she shakes her head. She gets up from his lap, taking a step back. 'Don't worry, I'll just keep my doors and windows locked.'

In a flash, he closes the distance between them. His hand settles possessively at the small of her back, bringing her even closer than before. 'You'll never, ever be a burden to me, Tara. Besides, I need you. I don't want to be alone tonight,' he says, before he brings his lips to hers, silencing her protests with a kiss.

A lane away from the beach, Noel's sunny yellow Goan villa is nestled between mango and coconut trees. It's lined by a charming *balcão*, a traditional Goan porch, and has a sloping red-tiled roof. Inside, the home flows from one room to another, with light spilling in through the large seashell windows and Venetian balconies with bougainvillea-covered wrought iron railings.

The decor is tasteful – antique Goan and rustic wooden furniture that fits perfectly with the red oxide tiled floor and earthy palettes of the walls, yet contrasts wonderfully with modern minimalist art and sculptures around the house.

'This place is gorgeous!' she says.

He smiles, 'It's our ancestral home, though I have added a few touches of my own to it.'

He guides her to a guest bedroom, with a massive antique four-poster bed, and doors that open to a swimming pool and gazebo.

'Meet you in the garden in half an hour?' he offers, placing her suitcase by a heavy wooden wardrobe.

Tara takes a long, hot shower before slipping into a sleeveless floral dress, leaving her face makeup-free and her curly hair wild for a change.

Noel is already waiting for her in the garden. He's freshly shaven and wearing a pale blue linen shirt with khaki pants, looking much more relaxed as he lounges on one end of a straw sofa with plush cushions. In front of him is a table with a massive vase full of summer flowers, scented candles and an ice bucket with a bottle of wine chilling in it.

He draws in his breath when he sees her, a dark fire burning in his eyes. 'I like you like this, without any makeup,' he whispers in her ear when she joins him on the sofa. Tara can already feel the butterflies fluttering in her stomach, as he hands her a glass of white wine.

He raises his in a toast. 'To Ana.'

'How did you meet her?' she asks him after she takes her first sip. She lifts up her legs to tuck them under her bum, but he grabs them gently, placing them on his lap instead.

'We go a long way back. Our dads knew each other – they were in the army together,' he says.

'Ah, so you're …'

'Half-Russian, yes. After his unit was disbanded, dad was never fully okay. He came down to Goa in the 1970s in search of what he called "spiritual salvation" … and then he found drugs,' Noel continues, playing with her toes. 'Goa was something else then. It was pure wilderness. Dad rented an old house on top of a hill, and started a fairly humble restaurant, with a couple of tables and chairs. It became quite popular, especially among Anjuna's hippies. It was doing well, but not well enough. He died when I was fourteen, and my younger brother Leo was about six – and he left us in huge debt. Our mother passed away four years later, and I had to take over the restaurant, and also take care of Leo. Luckily, I realized I had a knack for this thing.'

'You mean hospitality?'

'Knowing the right people, greasing the right palms,' he clarifies. 'The restaurant just kept growing after that. We started doing really well, and over the years, it turned into Club Coyote.'

'So where's Leo now?'

'He moved to Mumbai when he was seventeen. He runs a cafe there now.'

'Do you see him often?'

'Not enough,' he says, looking a bit wistful.

'What about your mom?' she asks.

'She was a local.'

A local.

'I am getting the vibe you weren't close to her either,' she says, trying to keep her tone light.

'I despised her,' he says bitterly. 'My dad insisted we keep her name. Being a local gives you a certain ease of access in business here. He was right, but I still hate it – or anything to do with her, really.

'Intimacy, trust … I struggle with these things. Oddly, I feel Coyote has insulated me from it even more. People don't know me or even see the real me, and sometimes I prefer that. To live a life that's solitary. To let them label me however they want. I find it easier to be surrounded by employees, hangers-on and vultures than friends. In fact, I am better at relationships that are transactional and emotionless, be it with employees or women.'

She feels a well of emotion rise up within her. 'What about your father? It sounds like you both loved each other.'

His face hardens into a mask, making him look like someone else, as he remains silent for a few seconds. And then it thaws, and he's Noel once again. 'You're right. Whatever unspoken thing we had, it was the closest I've ever felt to love in my life,' he whispers, and it breaks her heart.

In that moment, she vows to give him all the love she can possibly give him. All the love she feels she's never deserved herself.

The moonlight is casting a white spotlight on his face right now, and he's so unbearably handsome she feels she's sitting in a darkened theatre, watching a movie star on screen.

It feels like her whole life was a dress rehearsal for him. Like all those sleepless nights reading about dukes and Vikings and viscounts and earls – all those feverish dawns spent penning her fantasies about werewolves and vampires – were all building up to this.

It was all leading her to him. She had been waiting for him. No, she had manifested him.

Even as those words make Tara break out in goosebumps, even though her heart is racing a million miles a second, it feels a little too good to be true.

You really think someone like him could love you? Just look at yourself, Tara, the beast sniggers. *You're two different species, you fool. Wait till he realizes that. Wait till he sees how ordinary you are, and leaves like the rest of them did. Wait till ...*

The voice fades just as Noel's lips touch hers ever so gently.

'I am so glad to have you here,' he whispers against her lips, before claiming them with his. He tastes of white wine and all her dreams come true.

Just as he deepens the kiss, and she slips her hands into his hair, a deep slurring voice causes them to break apart and jump up from the sofa. 'Sorry to interrupt the makeout session,' it booms from behind them. 'Just thought I'd drop in and say hello to my big brother.'

12

It's still so disorienting to look at Leo. Tara tries not to stare at his scar, or his one unmoving eye, or the rest of his features that are exactly like his brother's. Instead, she fixes her gaze on his old faded black T-shirt that has two zombies locked in a passionate kiss under a death metal band logo, slowly lowering them to his ripped jeans.

'Well, well, well,' Leo says, grabbing the bottle of wine from the bucket and chugging straight from it. 'Looks like I'm crashing a date.'

'Leo, I am so happy to see you, brother,' Noel says, with a smile, as he gives Leo a warm hug. 'This is Tara. She's staying with me for a few days.'

Tara watches Leo rudely shove his brother's arms away, before he smirks at her. 'That's just lovely!' he says and plonks himself down on the sofa, taking another massive swig of the wine.

He stares at her unnervingly as he continues, 'Isn't this a great house, Tara? Noel's done a great job of painstakingly removing every single childhood memory from it. Which is great,' he says, leaning back and making himself comfortable, 'since our childhood really wasn't all that, was it Noel? It was pretty fucked up.'

The brothers exchange a look, and Noel forces a smile. He takes a seat across from Leo, and Tara joins him.

'How's Bombay?' he asks Leo, who is in the process of rolling a joint.

'Same old, same old,' his brother says, not even looking up.

'Cafe's doing well?' Noel presses on.

'Yeah, all thanks to your magnanimity, big brother,' Leo says sardonically.

'Ah, it was nothing. The least I could do,' Noel replies, refusing to take the bait. 'You've always been such a great baker. Tara, you gotta try one of his breads!'

Leo ignores him, slowly licking the end of the rolling paper to seal the joint. He brings out a zippo from his pocket to light it and takes a deep drag, exhaling the smoke right into Tara and Noel's faces.

'So, this thing between you two – it's for real?'

'What do you mean?' Tara asks, watching him take another, even deeper drag, and then hit them with another cloud of smoke.

'Noel likes to sow his wild oats all over Goa,' he replies. Then he smirks at his brother as he passes him the joint.

'Come on, stop trying to scare her away,' Noel says with a nervous laugh.

'Nah, I couldn't even if I tried. She's got it bad. Just look at her.' Leo smirks, making Tara squirm and want to disappear into the sofa or dissolve into the ground. 'But you have that effect on the ladies, don't you? You gotta teach me some of those tricks.'

'Leo, you're being rude,' Noel says, his voice deceptively calm, as he holds Tara's hand in a white-knuckled death grip. She tries to wiggle her fingers, afraid he might shatter some bones, but he doesn't even notice.

'Noel, my hand,' she finally squeaks in his ear. It seems to break him out of his trance.

'Oh,' he says, as he loosens his grip, grazing his lips against her knuckles in apology. To her utter horror, he then hands her the joint and excuses himself to get another bottle of wine.

Now she's alone with his psycho brother, who seems extremely pleased at her discomfort. He looks at her like a hunter about to finish its prey, prolonging the silence to make her squirm even more.

Unable to bear it any longer, she croaks out, 'Can I suggest something? Give it a break. Your brother loves you.' She realizes her hands are shaking when she brings the joint to her lips.

'Stay out of it,' Leo snaps.

'He's not doing well. Especially since Ana died. You know how close they were their whole lives. She was his *only family,'* she says, before realizing what she just said. 'Besides you, of course,' she tries to course-correct.

That seems to silence Leo for a while, a contemplative expression appearing on his face, like he's having some kind of a revelation.

'Check it out, this bottle is from dad's collection.' Tara's never been happier to hear Noel's voice. He's carrying a fancy bottle of wine in one hand, and a portable speaker in the other.

'Oh, yes, *that* guy,' Leo rolls his eyes.

'Cut it out, Leo,' Noel says, his voice carrying a warning.

His anger delights Leo, of course. He seems to enjoy nothing more than getting under Noel's skin.

'Oh, sorry, sorry,' he says. 'What I meant to say was, what a great dude. A rockstar. Noel's hero!'

The words land like blows, each one chipping away at Noel's composure. A muscle in his jaw clenches, then another, until his face sets into a mask. He looks like a tightly coiled spring, on the verge of snapping, every fibre of his being straining to hold back from attacking his brother.

Desperate to end this tension, Tara abruptly switches the subject. 'So, Leo, tell me more about this cafe of yours.'

Leo's smile widens. 'You mean the one Noel financed for me to assuage his own guilt?' He shakes his head, 'He's so much like dad in that sense.'

'Leo,' Noel says in a voice that's half-pleading, half-warning.

'What? You're just like him!'

'Come on, Leo. Not this again.'

'Okay, okay. I'll stop,' Leo says, throwing his hands up in the air as if to call for a truce. He leans over to grab Noel's phone from his hand, changing the song. Lively guitar chords fill the air in complete contrast to the current mood, as a male voice starts singing the famous Konkani song 'O Maria Pita Che'.

The blood drains from Noel's face, while Leo gets up and starts dancing.

'Come on,' he beckons Noel to join him. 'Mom loved this song! Remember how she used to dance to it?'

Noel ignores his brother, the rage now boiling to the surface. Tara can tell that that's exactly what Leo's aiming for.

'That poor woman,' Leo says to Tara in the same jovial voice as he shimmies towards her. 'Between him and dad, she didn't stand a chance.'

'Enough Leo!' Noel roars, shutting off the music.

There's a chilling silence in the air, as the brothers stand face to face. They look like they're about to throw blows. They're both so similar-looking and ripped in their own ways that Tara isn't sure who'd win the fight. A part of her wants to see them go at it and feels it might even be sort of hot, like a male version of the Shakira–Beyonce 'Beautiful Liars' video.

'I am sorry to call it a night, kitten,' Noel says, his gaze never leaving Leo's. 'But I think my brother and I need to have a talk.'

'Sure,' she says, only too happy to leave. She feels lightheaded as she stumbles along the corridors. *Wow.* She didn't realize how strong that joint was, or perhaps she went a little too hard on the wine. Either way, she feels her vision cloud a bit, and has to cling to the walls to keep herself upright.

She's so relieved when she finally makes it to the guest room, even as it starts spinning. She makes it to the bed just in time, passing out face-down on it.

Tara wakes up with her stomach rumbling. She's *starving*.

She doesn't know where the kitchen is, though – she doesn't remember seeing it during the home tour Noel had given her earlier in the day.

She wanders around the massive house that's dark and eerily silent, using her phone torch to light the path ahead of her as she peeks into every room. There's one with a pool table. Another with a gym. She reaches what looks like Noel's study, where a heavy mahogany desk with a leather chair sits imposingly in front of a floor-to-wall bookcase. *Oh, yay, a man who reads!* Tara thinks happily as she walks in. She shines a torch on his collection that's mostly limited to Russian classics, autobiographies of war generals and encyclopaedias. *Bo-ring!*

Suddenly, she feels the skin on her back prickle with goosebumps, as though she's being watched.

'Who's there?' she squeaks, shining her torch at the door with one hand, while fumbling for the light switch with the other. She presses all the buttons, and harsh white lights illuminate the room.

Her breath hitches in her throat, a gasp escaping from her lips as she sees a whole row of exotic animals staring down at her from the wall. Taxidermy shoulder mounts of a bear caught mid-growl, a hyena with a fanged, leery smile, a gorilla with its teeth bared in a snarl, a majestic deer with massive antlers. There are at least ten creatures regarding her with glittering eyes that still seem ... *so alive*. Their soulless faces make Tara want to scream. She backs away slowly, as though terrified that any noise could awaken them and tear her apart.

Run, her gut tells her, *something is wrong with this place, Tara* – just as her back hits the bookcase, hard. She hears a loud click. The bookcase separates from the wall, and she peers behind it to see a set of stairs leading into darkness.

For once, Tara decides to listen to her gut. She starts running until she reaches the garden, where she calls up Ahana.

Her sleepy voice answers. 'It's 3 a.m., Tara. Are you okay? Why haven't you picked up any of my calls?'

'I have to tell you something.'

'Can't it wait till the morning?' her groggy friend pleads.

'No,' she says, as she fills Ahana in on the past few days' events against her will.

'And so you moved into his house? Like, you hardly know this guy, Tara. What kind of person is best friends with a cult leader slash murderer slash werewolf?'

'It's complicated. They go a long way back.'

'His own brother hates him. And all that stuff about his relationship with his mother is creepy.'

'I just feel like we shouldn't judge him without knowing the whole story,' Tara argues, sinking into one of the chairs.

'Do you know how many police cases there are against him and his nightclub?' Ahana's voice is getting louder.

'Were you Googling him?'

'Of course, I Google all your boyfriends.'

'But he's not my boyfriend yet,' Tara clarifies, sounding a bit too wistful about it.

'*Tara!* Can we focus? I don't understand why you are still in Goa after that wolf attacked you. Living in this strange man's house. I mean, do you know anything about him? Does he care about the environment? Is he even a feminist?'

'Relax, Ahana. It's not what you are making it out to be. It's totally fine.'

'You called me, remember? I know that you know that this situation is messed up, too!'

'I know, but ...'

'You should get out, Tara. *Now.* You sound like you did that time. I can hear it in your voice. You're turning back into that person.'

'What person?'

'The delusional Tara. The fucked-up Tara. Don't act innocent with me. I was there in the hospital with you that night,' Ahana warns.

Tara squeezes her eyes shut at that, trying to fight the images flooding her brain. But it's too late. The coppery scent of her own blood fills her nose, the metallic taste of it in her mouth.

She's back in that room again. Her shaky bloody fingers dialling 100, as she wonders – *Am I overreacting?* – before her phone is ripped away from her hands and comes down onto her with the force of a fist. 'Hello? Hello? What's your emergency?' the operator says from its disintegrated remains. Panic tightens her chest as Tara whispers, 'My eye! I can't see ...'

Tara breathes in and out, forcing her eyes to shut tighter, forcing the images to leave. She imagines wrestling with them, pummelling them, then wrapping them up in a plastic bag and shoving them down harder and harder, back into the black box in the back of her brain.

'You know I don't like talking about that. Besides, it's been years since then. I learnt my lesson,' she tells Ahana in a shaky voice.

'I doubt it,' her friend's voice is an awful mix of pity and disgust, just like it was that night.

'Ahana, I already have a fucking mom, I don't see why you have to be such a hard-ass all the time too!' Tara's yelling now. Loud enough that she doesn't hear it creep up behind her. She's so drunk and mad, she barely registers its breath in her ear. It isn't until its wet drool drips on her neck that Tara turns around.

The wolf's furry hands are already around her waist. She drops her phone, screaming. '*Are you okay?*' Ahana yells back at her, though her voice is muffled by the grass. '*Answer me, Tara!*'

It's so close to her that Tara can see the creature isn't a wolf. No, it's something else entirely. It's a gorgeous mutation of nature or a mythical chimera. It's the glittering eyes of a panther over a snout of a wolf. It has the height of a grizzly bear and the girth of a silverback gorilla. It's something that was born or designed to eviscerate whatever was in its path.

Staring at it, at whatever this *being* might be, Tara feels a fear that's absolute, concentrated, profound and humbling ... like she's finally face to face with the terrifying beauty of death, with the hopeless void she's been crawling – no hurtling full-speed – towards, her whole life. And yet, even in this dying moment, her brain denies her the highlight reel of her life's best moments.

Instead, it fixates on an article she read as a child in her mother's old, dusty *Reader's Digest*, about a circus trainer whose finale act involved sticking his face inside a lion's mouth. Each night, the audience would sink into their seats, alarmed and fascinated. Not just by the lion and the spectacle, but also the man's hubris; at his confidence in the fact that the wild animal wouldn't hurt him simply because he had brought it up since it was a cub, fed it with his own hands and trained and tamed it with his expertise.

Until one day, during their routine finale act, the lion's tooth accidentally sunk into the man's neck, and it tasted blood. The problem was, it couldn't stop after that. It kept wanting more, until the man's face was all chewed up, and it left a gaping wound where his lips and nose should have been. They had included gruesome pictures of the trainer's injuries, as well as his face after reconstructive surgery. Skin sewed back on in a way that seemed too tight and wrong and just barely held together by angry red scars, with only a hole for a nose and a part of his lip still missing, revealing his bare upper teeth. They were branded into Tara's brain for life.

She shuts her eyes, her heart thudding as she waits for the beast to do the same to her; waiting to be mauled and chewed up ...

Seconds later, she opens her eyes just a little and sees that the creature's movements are a bit drowsy. It holds Tara clumsily, swaying from side to side. Her sense of self-preservation finally and reluctantly sputters to a start. She finds herself smashing the empty wine bottle on the table and stabbing the creature in its side with the broken, ragged edge.

It releases her, whimpering. Bending over, it lets out a howl that seems almost ... *human*. Before she can make sense of it all, Leo is behind her, yelling, 'Tara, go inside – *now*!'

Leo cradles the wailing beast in his arms, as Tara breaks into a run, not stopping till she's back in the guest room. Till her trembling hands lock the door.

Only then does she let herself sink to the floor, allowing herself to breathe and come to terms with what she just saw. And more importantly, what she just *smelt.*

She'd know that scent anywhere.

It was Noel's.

13

'Tara, let me explain,' she hears Noel's muffled voice outside her room the next morning. 'Let me in, please,' he begs, his hands hammering at the door of the guest bedroom in a steady, ominous rhythm.

'Go away,' she yells, her nervous heart ticking in her ribcage like an agitated rabbit likely to flip over and die if someone were to so much as whisper 'boo!'

'You're safe with me, Tara, I promise,' he says, and she wishes more than anything that she could believe him. But she's no longer sure of what lies on the other side of the door.

She feels the hair on her arms rise, as she recalls the otherworldly beast with glowing eyes – dead, blank and nothing like Noel's – from last night. The eyes of a creature that had no emotions or conscience, that knew no better than its evolutionary instincts or hunger.

Did he recognize her last night? Would he have hesitated to rip her apart even if he did? It didn't seem like it, and that's what scared her.

That and the fact that her stupid gut had already put two and two together a long time ago, and had been waiting for the rest of her body to finally catch up. It was him.

In fact, some mutinous parts of her body were still trying to pathetically feign disbelief. Her eyes refused to admit that the furry black body, with its enormous paws and talons, could ever be Noel's. Her ears, meanwhile, were refusing to believe that the snarls and growls could ever come from a human. Her nose, now a hostile witness, was trying to backtrack on whether the scent was really Noel's or not.

But he isn't human, is he? That's the problem! Her gut tries to prompt her.

Then what the fuck is he?

You know the answer to that, too, don't you, Tara? Her gut whispers ever so gently, trying to protect her skittish rabbit heart.

Shut up, Tara begs silently.

'Tara,' Noel says. 'I just need five minutes.'

'Okay,' she says, opening the door a smidge. 'You have fifteen seconds.'

Her defences melt the moment Noel's eyes – swollen and red-rimmed, filled with regret, repentance and a softness completely unlike the beast's – gaze into hers. Her belly gives way to something warm and molten.

It's Noel, *her* Noel.

He looks so ... beautiful and broken, human and vulnerable. He can't be what she thinks he is. He just cannot!

Oh, Tara, her gut sighs.

He reaches out to caress her hand, the one she's holding the door open with, interlinking their fingers and locking his eyes onto hers. Something familiar and unspoken passes between them, along with white hot streaks of electricity.

'Let me in, kitten,' he says in a voice so impossibly deep – a voice that even when apologetic, carries a seductive, commanding undertone she finds hard to resist or disobey. Tara finds herself melting. She's seconds away from puddling at his feet. 'Give me a chance to explain. And you can leave after that if you want.'

She nods, opening the door and letting down the last of her defences. He's standing there, shirtless as usual. It's embarrassing to admit that if Noel had hoped the six-pack would help warm her up to his apology, he was right. He flinches as he walks into the room, and Tara finally registers the big, bloody bandage on the side of his torso. He notices her watching.

'What was that last night? What did I see?' She's almost begging him to tell her all her fears are unfounded.

'You really did a number on me, didn't you?' he says instead, making his way towards her slowly, tentatively, wincing with pain each time he takes a step.

It was *him. He isn't even denying it anymore.*

She backs away from him slowly, still hoping he'll tell her another pretty lie today. Something digestible and comforting that will fit perfectly with all her fantasies of him, something that will help her sleep peacefully tonight.

Gaslight me, feed into my delusions, please, she tries to plead with him telepathically before he opens his mouth. *Please don't say ...*

'You know the answer already, Tara.'

She shakes her head, wanting to live in denial for as long as she can. Because he can't possibly be—

'A *werewolf*?' Tara squeaks as the back of her knees hit the bed, and she falls onto it. She stares at him, a slight shiver running down her spine, even though the idea of a werewolf sounds so stupid here in the daylight. She prays one last time that he'll laugh because she's said something so hilarious, outrageous and impossible.

Noel doesn't laugh. Instead, he looks at her earnestly, guiltily – and it's the only confirmation she needs. Running her hands through her hair, she hunches over, holding her stomach because it suddenly hurts with all this newfound knowledge.

He sits down next to her, and she recoils from the proximity. Noticing this, he says, 'To start with, I would never, ever hurt you. I have been within an inch of you so many times. If I had to hurt you, I would have done it by now.'

She's hunching even more now, trying to roll up into a ball like a defensive armadillo, rocking herself back and forth. 'You should have told me earlier. Why wait till now? Why wait till I'm in ...'

Love. She holds back that last word, along with her tears.

'Tara,' he says, voice so soft and yet rough at the same time. His fingers slide under her chin, forcing her to look up into his eyes, now filled with tears. 'This is what I was afraid of. *This* look on your face. I delayed the inevitable because I didn't want to scare you away.' His lips are so close to hers. She wants to bridge the gap, end the conversation, forget everything that just happened.

But he's already telling her the things she doesn't want to know. 'The truth is that I'm not a werewolf, but a Bodark. It's a warrior race that originated close to Russia. They were known for their ability to shapeshift. Some of our ancestors were even immortal. I am one of the last surviving ones ...

'In the fifteenth century, our community was banished, our lands taken away. The members lived a shadow existence. Many were executed in the trials that followed when they were lumped together with werewolves. The survivors had to change their names, learn how to blend in.

'Later, our people were hired by the Red Army as mercenaries and so many died on the battlefield. The Bodark unit was disbanded a few years after my dad joined, when our powers had become diluted due to inter-race marriages.'

It's too much information to comprehend in one go, but Tara still tries. 'So was your dad a Bodark, too? And what about Leo?'

'My father was one, but I only found out about a year before he passed away. That's when he began preparing me for my transition. As for Leo, you have to be born under precise conditions for the gene to kick in, so he isn't a Bodark. I don't know how I turned out to be one either, considering my dad married a local.'

Tara notices again how he uses that term to dismiss his mother. The hate reflected on his face makes her recoil. She tries to ignore it and prompts him, 'So, when did you first turn into, you know, the Bodark or whatever?'

'At fourteen.'

Then, she asks him point-blank, 'Did you really murder those women, like they say you did?'

He looks like she has just stabbed him on the other side of his torso. 'No! I would never do something like that. It was Ana. It was all Ana.'

'Wait, so she was a Bodark, too?'

He nods. 'That's why I had to always be around her. She wasn't lucky like me. At least I had my father to train me for whenever I would transition. She lost her father long before she knew what she was. She would have been worse, *so much worse,* had I not been there to control her.'

'I mean, would you even remember if you killed someone?' Tara argues, biting her lower lip. 'Are you a sentient werewolf?'

'*Bodark*,' he clarifies gently. 'Yes, I am aware of my actions, though I can't always control them. But Tara, I promise you, apart from a few ... *accidents* ... when I was younger, I've never hurt anyone. Not on purpose.'

Once again, Tara's body breaks into goosebumps, while her gut churns in warning.

'I can't believe that werewolves – Bodarks – actually exist. This whole thing is ridiculous!' she exclaims.

'You're the one who's made a living out of them,' he says with a weak smile, adding, 'Besides, I feel like you knew what I was. You just didn't want to come face to face with it.'

He's right. Some part of her always knew. If anything, it had made her want him *more*.

'And the moon and werewolves thing – is it all true?'

'We are at our most powerful when it's a full moon. Initially, that was when I would lose control. But I have spent years working on myself. With enough training and practice, it is possible to completely override your urges and live a somewhat normal life. That's what I was trying to help Ana with as well.'

'So, you know others ... like you two?'

'Yes, there are many like us back in Russia, but Ana was the only Bodark I've met in real life apart from my father.'

Clearing her throat to buy time, she says, 'You can understand why this may be a lot to take in.'

'There's no one holding you back, Tara. You can leave if you want,' he says, even though his hand had somehow found its way to hers during the conversation. His grip is like a vice.

'I think I should,' she tries to wriggle free. 'I mean, I just don't see how this is going to work out, you know?'

'Sure.' He lets go of her hand, his face hardening into that impenetrable mask again.

But she doesn't move. They sit there, silently and awkwardly, until she finally whispers, 'Sorry, Noel.' Even though his eyes are still cold and distant, his voice breaks just a little, as he asks, 'Can I just show you one last thing before you go?'

Tara nods. *I can give him this much, can't I?*

He leads her into his study. He presses on a thick and tattered rare edition of Mary Shelly's *Frankenstein* before the bookcase clicks open. He leads her down the stairs, opening the heavy iron door at the end. Behind it is a depressing room that's dark, dank and bare, nothing like the rest of the house. The grey cement walls are grimy and covered in muck and blood. It's like a mouldy prison cell. In one corner, she spots thick iron chains too big to restrain a human. They are clearly meant for him.

'This is where my mother tied me up after the first time I turned, and each time after that,' he says. 'Sometimes, she would leave me here for days.'

'Why are you showing me this?' she asks, tearing up at the thought of how young and afraid and confused he must have been.

'Because I want you to know you're not the first one to think that monsters like me don't deserve love.' His voice wavers again as he says that, and it breaks Tara's heart. She grabs hold of his hand.

'She said I scared her ... she didn't care how scared I was myself,' he says as Tara grips his hand even more tightly. 'I just wanted to help Ana – I wanted her to have someone, because I had no one.'

It strikes her now why he chose *Frankenstein*. The book must remind him of himself. There are far too many parallels between him and the tragic literary creature: they were both born into a world that rejects them, where they were labelled as 'horrifying' and 'grotesque' and forced to live a life of isolation and abandonment for no fault of their own.

Tara can feel tears streaming down her face as she whispers, 'I am so sorry.'

He wraps her in a fierce hug. 'It's okay, kitten. You don't owe me anything.'

Maybe it's the fact that *he* is comforting *her*, but his words make Tara sob even harder.

'I write werewolf romance novels!' she bawls, hiccupping as she continues, 'I mean, if there's anyone who should be able to understand and get past this, it's me ... I just didn't expect it to be so terrifying. I mean I thought I was going to die last night.'

He turns into a beast against his will, Tara! You're just going to leave him because of something he can't help? Wow! Who's the real monster here?

'It's okay,' he says, pressing his lips against her forehead as she clings to him. 'I didn't anticipate falling in love with you either.' His voice is soft and caressing, and she feels him smile. 'I mean, I tried my best not to. I did everything in my power not to, in fact. But you turned out to be quite hard to resist.'

'You didn't anticipate *what*?'

He looks at her, confused, not realizing what he just said.

'You *love* me?' She can barely breathe with the butterflies warring in her stomach.

She waits for him to deny it, to say she heard the word wrong, but he is looking at her in a way he hasn't before. It takes her breath away. 'I have loved you since the day I saw you, kitten,' he whispers. His lips claim hers in a kiss that's possessive, like he's staking his claim on her. She kisses him back just as fiercely.

Still, she can't stop thinking about that moment when the lion switched, the moment it tasted blood and knew it would never go back. The moment the trainer realized – all too late – that it wasn't in the creature's nature to be tamed.

They are lying in the grass in Noel's garden, enveloped in a silence that amplifies the sounds of the crickets and frogs and her own thudding heart. It feels like they are the last people on a planet that's upside down. It's strange how comfortable she feels in this new world, where the lines between fiction and reality have been blurred. How at home she is with this man lying beside her, who is a little bit of both – fiction and reality.

How could I even have feared him in the first place? she wonders as she snuggles closer to Noel now. He is so perfect, he could very well be a figment of her imagination like he had sprung out of the crevices of her mind. The parts of it that are as dark and unknown and occasionally terrifying as the ocean.

His arms tighten around her from behind; their legs intertwine, and his lips graze her nape ever so gently. She feels safer than she has ever been, like a baby swaddled in a blanket.

At this moment, she and Noel no longer have secrets.

She feels like fifteen-year-old Tara in her Winnie-the-Pooh night suit – it's as if she is lying next to a hero from the books she used to read then. She's left wondering once again how someone can be so impossibly handsome, like the men on the covers that she'd hide with newspaper. His black kurta is doing a terrible job of covering his chiselled chest, and she feels an uncontrollable urge to run her hands all over it. She's obsessed with each strand of his long, unruly hair; fascinated by every pore of his skin. Each part of him feels so intimate and familiar and strange and fascinating that she's scared of her own desire to devour him at this very moment.

Her heart full and her head spinning from the bottle of wine they'd shared, she finds her tongue loosening up. 'You know what's really stupid? I read tons of romance novels growing up. But my favourite part wasn't the first time the characters met or when they kissed or even when they ... you know ...'

Noel grins at her newfound prudishness as she plays with the button on his kurta, and prompts, 'Then what?'

'It was the author's bio on the sleeve of the book jacket. The one that read: "The author lives with her husband and two cats in some hill station or Goa." That's the romantic ending I always wanted for myself. I wanted what was in the book and on its jacket, too.'

Their noses are now touching. He says, 'Now you have me. Not bad, Miss Tandon. You tamed the beast just like your heroines.'

It's Tara's turn to grin, as she moves away and lies with her back on the grass, looking at the stars.

'What made you obsess over werewolves in the first place?'

'It's a great literary metaphor for wrestling with your inner demons, maybe?' she shrugs, turning just in time to see his raised eyebrow. Grinning again, she gives him the more honest and mortifying answer. 'Okay, fine, it's because they're sexy in the most archaic way. A symbol of man at his most alpha: bestial or brutish, lacking any moral core or control. But also, someone who will love you and protect you. I think women secretly like that.'

'Brutish men with no morals or self-control?' he teases, turning onto his side to face her.

She loves the way he looks at her. Intensely, intimately, in a way that feels illegal – like she's some kind of a goddess or a meal he's been starved for. No matter how much it makes her blush and shrink away, she also finds herself revelling in his gaze. Like Gundi, her parents' cat, when she discovers a warm patch of sunlight to lie in. Tara finds herself wanting to purr and stretch the same way; to lie on her back with her belly exposed to him.

'No, being wanted in that uncontrollable way. There's something hot about being overpowered by something bigger than you, isn't it? Relinquishing all control?' Tara gets up and shakes the grass out of her hair. She's a bit worked up, as she always is when defending her books. 'That's what *they* don't seem to get about the books. Like, you don't have to be so literal about it. I mean, I'm a feminist who believes in consent and all that. But bodice rippers were always meant to indulge a side of us that didn't need to be "proper", a part that was dormant and base and hidden. All I want to do is create a forbidden fantasy. A world free of morals and hang-ups for you to live out that fantasy in.'

He's looking at her in a strange way that makes her feel self-conscious. Maybe her ramblings are too much, even for him.

'I mean, I'm not saying I don't have unresolved issues, I totally do,' she tries to course-correct.

'So monsters are just a metaphor for you?' he asks

with that same strange look. 'Do you think you can handle the real thing?' There is a challenge in his voice.

The black box strains and struggles in the back of her brain but she continues to smile, shrugging, 'Of course. I've dealt with monsters my whole life. I attract them, and somehow end up being attracted to them in return – like a moth to a flame, in fact.'

His expression changes instantly to the one she loves the most – the naughty schoolboy.

'Maybe I am not a monster then. Because the first time I saw you, I didn't expect to fall in love with you at all,' he teases.

'Because I wasn't a blonde with big boobs?' she throws back at him.

'No, because of this very cocky attitude.' He tries to look serious as he says it, but his dimples betray him. 'You have this strange ability to piss me off and turn me on at the same time.'

'Yes, all your negging has the same effect on me, too.'

Laughing, Noel pulls her back down onto the grass, until they're lying facing each other, with barely any space between them. Tara's heart starts racing as the laughter leaves his eyes. His voice a fierce growl, he says, 'The truth is you did attract me like a moth to a flame. When I found out about your books, it was like a sign ... No matter how hard I tried, I just couldn't stay away. And I did try so fucking hard. I wanted to protect you, not just from Ana, but myself, too.'

'But it was cosmically inevitable!'

'A bit dramatic, no?'

'I know, but isn't all this so wonderfully dramatic? I love that we're beyond the laws of fantasy and reality. The lines between madness and magic are blurring. It's like you're *my* monster, and I am Frankenstein!' she whispers fiercely. Tara is mesmerized as she half-imagines his eyes glowing like the beast's. They change back to normal an instant later.

Tracing the injury she gave him on his torso, she asks, 'Does it hurt?'

His eyes continue to smoulder. 'Not as much as the pain of losing you would have.'

She finds herself blushing, almost purring, while he stares at her. Unable to meet his eyes anymore, she buries her face into his chest and whispers, 'I like this you.'

'This me?'

'The you that is vulnerable, open.' She looks up at his handsome face again, and traces her fingers along his jaw and then his lips.

'Great,' he smiles against her fingertips. 'Now that you know everything about me, you can finally stop with the interrogation.'

'What interrogation?' she says, trying her best to look innocent.

'Are you kidding me? I was half-expecting you to start waterboarding me if you didn't get the answers you wanted!'

'Shut up,' she punches him on his arm this time. 'Besides, I do have a couple more questions, on behalf of my best friend Ahana.'

He groans as she straddles him, though his hands are already slipping into her Winnie-the-Pooh bottoms. 'Do you care about the environment?' she asks, not giving him a chance to answer before her lips find his. 'And are you a feminist?' She swallows his reply with her kiss.

14

It's outside her door.

Threatening to break it down.

Tara is leaning against the door with her full weight, the last of her defences. She's chewed-out and hollow; a festering wound, a walking zombie – there's nothing left for it to devour.

The maggots have already found her. It's only a matter of time before she gets eaten alive and whatever remains dissolves into the earth.

But it snarls and roars, not willing to let that happen.

It wants to be the one to finish her.

Instead of running away from the inevitable, Tara opens the door, forcing herself to confront his beautiful face and still-imposing frame. She whispers, 'Adi?'

This is why she doesn't like to remember him. Why she keeps him locked up in the box at the back of her brain.

Because every time she looks at him, she has to relive the whole experience in slow motion. Her brain prolongs each excruciating second; magnifying his anger, her own helplessness, the taste of blood and terror in her mouth.

She watches the phone come at her yet again, but it takes its time. She hears something in her body crack, remembering how the adrenaline coursing through her veins had made her oblivious to the pain back then. How she had felt vulnerable and invincible at the same time, even as he had continued to strike her.

That's the shameful truth of it. She didn't feel small and powerless that night. Those feelings had hit her belatedly, long after her physical recovery.

The truth is she didn't even fight back – in fact, a part of her had wanted *to push him to the edge, to test both their breaking points. She was curious to see how far he could really go and how much she could truly handle.*

In her head, it was still a power game, because she refused to believe how much the dynamics were skewed. She was desperate to get it over with, so that the anger would dissipate. When it did, she knew he'd assure her that she was really The One.

That she had always been The One.

And just like she had before, she'd diligently black out what happened. Scratch over the memory with a pen again and again and again, till she couldn't see it; till it joined all the other ugly scrawled-over moments in her brain.

Neither of them had really anticipated her landing up in the hospital that night, or the surgeries that followed.

The Therapist would later call these acts – of overwriting the incidents, of fleeing her body entirely while they were happening – 'dissociation'.

The Therapist would tell her that she had been protecting Adi by not telling anyone what he was, while he had been building up her tolerance to his escalating violence.

That he was lying through his teeth each time he told her he blacked out 'with the rage and the drugs, babe'.

She remembers how he'd say, 'You know me. You know the real *me'.*

She'd nod, even though she wasn't quite sure what she was agreeing to. She knew two of him – Dr Jekyll and Mr Hyde.

And she didn't know which one was really him.

When he had towered over her that night, one last time, she was afraid he'd become Mr Hyde for good. That Dr Jekyll would never return. The beast had decided it no longer wanted to play nice.

Suddenly, a voice calls out to her from far away.

Tara ...

TARA!

'What?' she snaps groggily from Noel's bed. Except there's no Noel next to her.

Seated by her feet is Leo. The blazing sun through the window makes his scars look angrier, while his glass eye refracts the sunlight directly into her face.

She squints before rubbing her eyes, and sulking at him, 'Whatever this is, can it wait? Noel and I were up all night talking, and now I need my beauty sleep.'

She dives back into her pillows, tugging the blanket over her head.

He pulls it off her. 'Hurry up. Start packing your bag. He'll be done with gym soon. We don't have a lot of time.'

'Why, what's the time? Wait, where's my phone?'

'He probably has it.'

'Who?'

'Noel.' He is speaking slowly, as though talking to a five-year-old with limited comprehension skills, and it offends her greatly.

'Well, can he give it back? I need to call Ahana, my best friend, or she'll worry.'

'He's probably already told her something to pacify her,' Leo says. Tara notices for the first time since she woke up that something isn't right about him. He's talking too fast and his body language is creeping her out, too. His shoulders are hunched and his eyes shifty – the human equivalent of how Gundi's back arches up unnaturally high, and her tail gets all slanty when she senses a predator.

'What the hell are you talking about? What's wrong, Leo?' she asks, now fully awake.

She still doesn't know if she likes or hates Leo, but her gut has come to trust him. It's a pity because the rest of her body wants to immediately reject the information he gives her next.

'Tara, listen to me carefully. Noel's dangerous. Very, very dangerous.'

'What? Are you talking about the werewolf thing? I know. It's alright, I accept him for who he is.'

He looks at her funny before switching back to his talking-to-a-five-year-old voice, 'Well, that's great, but you're still in danger.'

She laughs, though even to her, it sounds nervous and deranged. 'I don't know if you know this, but I wrote a book called *Wild Nights with the Werewolf*. I am not scared of Noel. I love him. Don't worry, I got this!' She's aware of the plastic doll-like smile that's appeared on her face but can't seem to wipe it off.

'Tara, I know you wrote those books, and more importantly, *he* knows you wrote those books. Trust me. That's how he found you in the first place.'

'Found me?'

'He's been stalking you.'

'He's been *stalking* me?' Tara repeats, letting out another forced giggle.

'And conning you.'

'But, why?'

'Because even cold-blooded killers get lonely? And because in his warped head, he thinks you understand him? Although I am now beginning to see why he chose you in particular.' He means it as an insult, but Tara feels like she is too dumb to get the joke – even if she's the punchline.

'Cold-blooded ... what?' She feels hungover, even though she isn't really hungover. No, she's just exhausted from attempting to figure out what he's trying to say.

Leo sighs. 'Look, I know the story he told you. Our mom was abusive, our dad was a part of some werewolf army unit.'

'The Bodarks,' Tara corrects him.

'Never mind that,' he says impatiently. 'The point is that he was lying. He borrowed the whole thing from a fucking video game. He was obsessed with it as a kid.'

'What?' Tara feels like she has just been slapped in the face.

'He isn't actually a werewolf, Tara.'

'Wait, what do you mean?' For the second time in two days, Tara feels the ground shift beneath her feet. It makes her want to throw up. 'That can't be! I saw the fucking beast with my own eyes, remember?'

Leo leaves her sitting on the bed alone for a couple of minutes before he returns with what looks like a massive dead animal in his arms. When he dumps the bloody carcass in front of her, she screams.

'Relax,' he says. 'It's a costume.'

Tara reaches out for it, fighting the urge to recoil, and runs her hand through the fur tentatively. Once she's sure it's not going to hurt her, she gingerly turns the costume over to see the animal's face. She recognizes it immediately. It's the face that's been lurking outside her window, the one she saw two nights ago.

'It's real wolf pelt, bear skin and some other animal parts. He's stitched them all together. He had this whole taxidermy phase as a kid; now it makes sense,' Leo says from what feels far away.

Tara thinks of Noel's study, the lifeless animals on its wall.

'In the video game that he was obsessed with, the soldiers used to wear something like this,' Leo is saying now.

Tara can't get over how incredibly real it looks – like a beast in hibernation. She could swear she saw its belly rise, as though it might still be breathing. As if it could still spring to life at any moment, to lunge at her and maul her to death.

Next to the costume is a gun. She looks at Leo questioningly.

'It's the gun he killed Ana with.'

'Why? Was it because she was a Bodark?'

'Like I said, there is no such thing as a Bodark, Tara.'

'But he told me—'

'He was *lying.*' Leo takes a deep breath before he continues, 'When I read about the first murder – all those people talking about spotting a werewolf – it didn't sit right with me. Knowing my brother's past, his history, it was too much of a coincidence. I know exactly what that man is capable of. That's why I left Goa in the first place.

'I tried to ignore the news, but then I read about a second murder, and a third – all tied to the same fucking animal. I couldn't sleep knowing that he could be behind them. I just had to come here and see for sure, if only to silence my own conscience.

'Of course, it's not like he would come right out and admit it to me. But I knew if I got him wasted enough, triggered enough, I could bring out that side of him. After all, who can push Noel's buttons better than me?'

'Oh, that's what you were doing last night,' Tara says slowly. *It all makes sense now.*

'It's been years since I have seen him like this. After mom died, he was the picture of calm. But the man I saw last night is nothing but a ticking time bomb.'

Leo's words make Tara's heart pound, even as she

hears herself say, 'I just can't believe it. There has to be some sort of an explanation—'

He hands her his phone, and she finds herself transfixed by the video playing on it. It's Noel, dressed in the linen pants he was wearing two nights ago, passed out against the wall of the basement behind the bookcase. Slowly, he starts to wake up and thrash around, whipping himself into a frenzy. He begins to growl like an animal. His body language becoming less and less human, and more and more wolf-like.

She waits and waits and waits for the hair to sprout, for Noel's face to turn into a wolf's, for the fangs and the claws and the beastly eyes that have haunted her for so long to appear. But that doesn't happen.

Because he remains human the whole damn time.

15

The first time Tara had become aware of her scary ability to twist reality in her mind had been with Adi.

He was smooth, too smooth. And much too handsome, too. She knew he was out of her league, and he liked to remind her of it in his own subtle ways. He'd diss her books: 'predictable, mushy ... it's not really literature, Tara. You could do better.'

Then her clothes. 'Do you have to dress like a man? What's with the baggy shit?'

Her laughter. 'It's too loud and besides, your teeth are too big.'

Her personality. 'Why do you have to air out your idiotic opinions in front of my friends like that? Do you really need to advertise what a bimbo you are to them, too?'

Her body. 'Do you really need those fries, Tara?', 'I can't believe how much you've let yourself go,

Tara', followed by 'I don't think I am attracted to you anymore, Tara.'

It is hard to remember now who told the bigger lies between them first. Did he trap her first with his sweet talk, all sticky like molasses? Or was she already waiting to absorb him into her endless void; her fake personality deceptive and bottomless like quicksand?

'I mean, you led me to believe you wanted to be a real writer, that you cared about fitness. You were anything but this depressed blob when I met you,' she remembers him saying.

The point is that they were both liars and storytellers, who'd go to any lengths to protect their shared delusion, their folie à deux.

The point is that when she did try to leave, he reminded her, 'Look at yourself, love. Who else will have you?'

That was when she had perfected her stupid plastic 'nothing is wrong' smile. Like a little five-year-old obsessed with her little plastic dollhouse, protecting her little plastic relationship from Ahana's 'I don't like the way he talks to you's and 'Don't let him control you's and 'You're better than this, Tara'.

She was proud of the alternate reality she had constructed in her head. Of the version of him she'd built painstakingly from scratch, to live inside this parallel world; one that went perfectly with an imaginary version of herself.

She didn't even realize the reality of what they had become until it all came crashing down.

She has that same bad feeling right now, as Leo stops the video.

'Make no mistake, he would have killed you had I not been there. That's why I locked him in the basement, but he escaped.'

Because Tara left the door open. There's that taste in her mouth again, of blood and terror. 'I don't get it. So he's mentally unwell?' she asks. 'Why does he believe he is a werewolf?'

'He had a rough childhood, and blanked out most of it from his mind,' Leo sighs. 'Like the parts where our dad hit our mom ruthlessly ... That's all gone.'

'He never mentioned anything about that.'

He smirks, 'Exactly. All he remembers is how our mother shot our father.'

'She ... *what*?' Tara's hands fly to her face in horror.

'It was in self-defence, but he could never be convinced of that. In Noel's eyes, his *dada* could do zero wrong.' Leo is still smirking. At this point, it feels like his smirk is as much a defence mechanism as Tara's plastic smile. 'Do you know he actually blamed our mother for getting hit? For being "weak"? For never leaving dad?'

He sits down at the edge of the bed, his head falling into his hands. 'It's not all Noel's fault, of course. Dad indoctrinated him young. Mom tried, I mean, *really* tried, to get to him. To convince him that he was living in some parallel reality. But now I can't help but feel like he inherited that gene of cruelty from my father. That has to be why they were so close in the first place. Dad was a vile man – cold and calculating – a bloody sociopath.'

He looks over at Tara, and continues, 'Long story short, Noel never really forgave mom. In fact, he was so scarred from watching dad die like that, he never completely recovered. Something went horribly wrong with him that night. I think he was in denial, and desperate to change the narrative in his head.

'He'd spend hours locked in his room, playing that video game, and it just kept becoming more real to him. Before I knew it, he already believed all those things about our father being from a Russian werewolf bloodline or whatever, and I couldn't convince him otherwise. Mom and I, we were afraid of him. I mean, he had always had anger issues like dad, but it got much darker.'

'Darker?'

'We'd hear him "turn" in his room. Roaring and breaking things. He'd be gone all night, or for days at a time. We'd hear about animal attacks in nearby villages. We knew it was him, but we never had any proof.

'Then he did this to me.' Leo smiles joylessly, pointing to his face. Tara stares at his scars. 'I told him that I knew it was him, that I was going to the police, and he ripped out my fucking eye.

'He felt very guilty, of course. Said he'd never forgive himself. That it was hard for him to control himself when the Bodark took over. We had no choice but to chain him up on full moon nights after that. Still, I thought he was sick and needed our help, but my mother never trusted him. He was no longer a skinny fourteen-year-old boy; he was getting so much bigger than her. Despite him getting therapy and medication, she was paranoid that he was going to kill her. She thought whatever he had become was her own fault. Her guilt got to her before he did, and she shot herself, just like she had dad.'

He takes a deep breath, as if steeling himself to continue. 'I was still a kid back then, barely ten years old. And Noel stepped up to the plate. He took over the restaurant and he really took care of me, too. There were no more attacks or suspicious incidents for a while. Still, I couldn't wait to get out of here. He always made me uneasy, and I blamed him for what happened to mom. I left to study in Mumbai as soon as I could, and a few years later, once Coyote started doing well, he helped me open my cafe.

'All these years, I honestly thought Noel had gotten the help he needed, but when the Bliss girls began to turn up dead, I knew I was wrong. Something must have set him off, maybe when he met Ana and she introduced him to Bliss. These women reminded him of our mother. He probably saw them as "weak", too. He specifically chose the ones he thought no one would miss.'

Tara shivers. 'But he promised he would never hurt me. He said he loved me,' she whispers.

'He's a sociopath, Tara, just like our father was. I don't think he's capable of love or anything resembling it,' Leo says. 'He's good at mimicking our feelings and making us believe it. Look at what he did to Ana. He said he loved her, too.'

Tara shakes her head. 'No, what we shared was real. I could feel it. Look, maybe he's just unwell. There has to be some solution to this. Medication, therapy, love.'

He looks at her funny again – like maybe she could use some medication and therapy, too. 'He is a murderer, Tara. It's not the werewolf you should be afraid of, but the human Noel. It's time to put this to an end. Let's get out of here.'

She nods, a single tear running down her face. 'I feel like such a fucking idiot.'

Leo tries to console her, 'He is a skilled manipulator. He knows people's weaknesses. He's studied you carefully. Everything up to this moment was carefully choreographed by him. He made you fall in love with him.

'You know, when he did this to me – the night after he ripped my face apart – he told me he has no control whenever the wolf takes over. But now I know it's an excuse to let out his real self. The monster he truly is.'

The door opens behind them.

Tara's gut warns her to *run, run, run*. But it's already too late. She hears the blunt *chuck, chuck, chuck* of the knife slicing into human skin, penetrating muscle and tissue for what feels like ages. She opens her mouth to yell, but no sound comes out as she watches Leo's body fall to the ground, his glass eye rolling across the floor and stopping just by her feet. She stares at his empty eye socket, feeling like she's about to throw up as his blood pools, expanding achingly slowly, until her feet and ankles are bathed in it. She notices that his glass eyeball is all bloody, too.

While the rest of her body is paralyzed by fear, her eyes follow Noel's *chappal*-clad feet wading through the blood, making sick squelching noises and tracking footprints. She sees the knife in his hand, and waits for him to come for her next, but instead he gathers the suit and the gun, and walks away. She hears a heavy clunk outside the door and the rattle of chains, followed by the sound of his fading footsteps.

She must have passed out from shock, Tara realizes as she wakes up in the same spot, still in her Winnie-the-Pooh pyjamas covered in Leo's blood. It's morning, and the floor, now bathed in sunlight, has been wiped clean. Leo and his glass eye and his pool of blood have been replaced by a plate of croissants and coffee from Shakti Shack. A long-stemmed rose lies next to them on the tray like some sort of a cruel joke.

She spots Noel's chappals from the corner of her eye, before he comes closer and crouches beside her. A voice – her own – is coming from the phone in his hand. She recognizes the video playing on it: a talk she gave a year ago on the evolution of the 'Werewolf Hero'.

'*Werewolves have historically been an effective metaphor for insanity, or the moral darkness and natural cruelty lurking beneath our human surface,*' on-screen Tara is saying. '*But unlike medieval folklore, in modern-day romances, the werewolf takes the form of the marginalized beast. Misunderstood, irrational and bestial ... but innately noble. Someone to sympathize with.*'

'This is when I first fell in love with you,' Noel says, next to her. 'When I saw this video.'

He's wearing nothing but his basketball shorts, sweaty like he's just come back from a workout. Like he wouldn't let something as small as him murdering his brother get in the way of his usual morning routine.

She sees that he's no longer wearing a bandage over the wound she had given him. In fact, it looks like nothing more than a papercut.

In the background, Tara drones on. '*In Ruth Marger's* Tryst with the Werewolf, *for example, the author is inspired by the mating rituals of wolves in the wild, who are known to be monogamous. She also draws from myths related to wolves and werewolves. How they can mark their mates, smell their scent for miles.*'

'I marked you, too, the moment I saw you. I knew there was something different about you,' Noel says, his eyes glistening. 'It's like you saw me for who I really was. For the first time, I felt like someone recognized me.'

'*The thrill of the forbidden, in the safe realm of fiction, is perhaps what makes the werewolf such a popular figure*,' Tara continues in the background, while Noel entreats her softly, 'I'm sorry to scare you, kitten. But you know I had to do that, right?'

'As in murder your brother and Ana?' Tara asks.

'They were both threatening to blow my cover,' he says, as though that's a fitting reason. 'Do you know what the police would do to someone like me?'

'You shouldn't have done it,' Tara looks away from him. The words come out shaky, just like her breath. 'He said you're going to kill me.'

She can tell he doesn't like what she's said because his body language changes the moment he hears it. Bringing his face closer to hers, he scrunches up his features until he no longer looks human. Like an aggressive wolf about to attack its prey. Yet, his voice remains casual, calm and human. 'It only goes to show how little you know me. I would never hurt you. The Bodark would never, ever hurt you.'

Tara can't wrap her head around the horrifying contrast between his tone and expression, as he continues in that same voice of reason, 'Do you know what twenty years of suppression can do to a person, Tara? I'm sick of it!'

His hand comes towards her, and she closes her eyes, anticipating violence. Instead, she feels his fingers stroke her cheek, 'I'm glad I don't need to hide anymore with you, Tara.'

She opens her eyes and finds herself staring directly into his grey ones. She can't spot a shred of humanity in them. Tara realizes now why it had always felt wrong with him. Just like Leo had told her, Noel had been mimicking her romantic heroes, especially the ones from her own books, this whole time.

Those smouldering looks. That cheesy nickname. *Kitten.*

He was just trying to be who she wanted him to be. The whole time she was falling head over heels in love, he had been simply playing a part.

She realizes now that it didn't even matter that he was a terrible actor, because she wanted to believe it so badly. In fact, she was the perfect victim – just like, or probably worse than, all those women in the documentaries about dating app swindlers and scam artists. Just like them, she'd have given those fraudulent men millions, too. She had fallen for every one of Noel's tricks. She would even have forgotten everything Leo told her the next morning and made up her own excuses on behalf of Noel, had he given her the chance.

How could he still have fucked up? All he had to do was hold up his end of the bargain! Killing his own brother last night, in front of her eyes, was hands down the dumbest move he could have made. How could she still make herself believe he could ever love her, when he could dispose of his brother and forget about him the next morning? She realizes, deep down, that she's not mad at Noel for deceiving her, but for doing such a terrible job of it.

Now Tara has no choice but to face this monster in front of her; to see him for what he really is.

She must confront the fact that he's no magical beast from her books, but everything Leo told her that he is – a killer and that deranged man in the video.

The wolf in human clothing.

But instead, she does the next best thing. She tries to let him down the easy way. 'I just ... I don't think this is going to work out,' she stutters.

'Oh. Well, I am disappointed. I thought you saw me. The real me,' he says, his body language becoming less human with each passing second.

'I don't know the real you,' Tara whispers.

'Don't lie. You've always known. You wanted me this way, *begged* for it.'

'No, Noel.'

She isn't sure if he's even listening to her anymore. Instead, he walks to the mirror, and as he gazes into it – at himself – he looks strange and unnatural, like an animal standing on its hind legs.

'Other women? They get scared of the Bodark. Sometimes, I need to knock them right out or do worse if the ladies protest too much,' he shrugs, running a hand over his six packs and biceps, freshly pumped after his gym session. 'But you're not like them, are you, kitten? You can handle the Bodark.'

Tara feels like she is about to throw up. 'What are you even talking about?'

'*Oh, I wish I could bottle up his danger ... the thrilling promise of violence sent shivers down my spine*,' Noel's voice mimics a little girl's as he spits out the familiar lines. He switches to his own as he adds, 'I read all your drafts. You're just like me.'

'You're wrong. I am nothing like you. I would never hurt anyone.'

That makes him turn around. With a cruel smile, he says, 'No, because you let them hurt you instead.

That's why we work, kitten. I am the werewolf of your dreams and fantasies. The ones that have been making you wet since you were a little girl. You're fucked up and twisted inside, like me. You just refuse to own it.'

Noel's right, of course. She is *fucked up and twisted and masochistic. And never more than when she was with Adi. She remembers how she had whittled herself down to nothingness for him, taking pride in how her ribcage pressed against the surface of her skin, how her collarbones threatened to poke out of what remained of it. She was so proud of her chicken-like arms, of her skinny legs. Her smile, on the spare occasions she did smile, was almost grotesque, like the bug-eyed woman from the Momo Challenge. She couldn't bear to look at herself in pictures from then for too long now, afraid she'd come out of them to haunt herself,* The Ring-*style.*

She remembers how she never told a soul that she had cheated her way to the perfect body for him. Sometimes, she'd imagine breaking protocol, grabbing their hands and pleading like a hostage, 'Please, I need help. My last meal was ice cubes, and my feet are blistered from my twelve-kilometre morning runs. Call someone, quick, hurry!'

She imagined them squirming in response, trying to awkwardly get rid of her.

She knew she was broken and damaged beyond repair.

Her body, all bones and scarred with stretch marks, felt like a newborn's – naked, vulnerable, with no evolutionary instinct yet. And worse, she continued to see the old her in the mirror.

Yet, she never told Adi that her appetite wouldn't go away. Along with it came a new hunger, to prove she wasn't her *anymore.*

She was grateful for Adi's scraps of acknowledgment, the hint of the slightest attraction in his eyes.

Eyes that seemed to say: 'You're someone else now. Someone new and shiny and worthy of love.'

That stink of the old her lingered though, no matter how hard she tried.

Though she was confident that she had managed to sever herself from her body, the old Tara continued to call out to her every night, like a phantom limb.

That's what her worst fears boiled down to. That's who hid under her bed and at the back of her closet – her self.

Until all she was reduced to was smoke and mirrors and cleverly timed distractions to hide the effort it took to not be her; to be anything but her.

And while she was just a handful of rabbits in a magician's hat, he was pure unadulterated rage.

She'd seen them then, too. Those dazzling things they call red flags. And yet she'd served her brittle and broken self to him on a platter. Let him tell her it was always her fault.

Let him constantly remind her of it, repeat it like a lesson. First with his words, then with his hands.

Ugly, worthless, talentless – *the words were branded on her skin, and still flared red after all this time.*

For whatever it's worth, she tries to appeal to Noel now. 'You're not a werewolf or a Bodark, Noel. Your brother, he told me everything.'

She knows she shouldn't have said it the moment she sees his eyes go dark. 'What did you just say?' he demands, in a low and chilling voice that gives her goosebumps.

He leans over and grabs her throat ever so tenderly with one hand, pushing her gently to the wall. 'You're not well, but you can get help,' she gasps, as his grip gets tighter with every word, until it is all but choking her.

'Shut up!' he yells, lifting her up and shaking her like a rag doll. 'Shut the fuck up!'

He brings his face closer to hers and whispers, 'Say that again, and I'll show you exactly what this beast is capable of.'

He releases her and watches her fall to the floor, crumpled into a sobbing heap by his feet.

16

'He said you were a fucking bitch, and then he grabbed you by the throat.'

The words sound almost benign when The Therapist says them so gently, so clinically.

'Later, he hit you on the side of your head with your phone, resulting in a cranial fracture and you almost losing your eye.'

She continues to walk Tara through the crime scene from a month ago, recounting the violence that Adi had inflicted on her in a tone that's dry yet compassionate at the same time. It distances Tara from everything that happened, while making her feel sorry for herself, too, for the first time.

'Do you really believe him when he says that he did it because he "lost control"?' The Therapist then asks.

Tara feels like this question is a test, and she already knows her answer is the wrong one. That's probably why it comes out all awkward, like a ramble. 'I believe him when he says he didn't mean to. He's genuinely a good guy! Like deep down, I know he still loves me. When it's good, we connect on this level ... that's almost spiritual, you know? Our chemistry is the most organic I have ever felt. We have the same worldview, sense of humour, our wavelengths match so perfectly. It's exactly like the love they describe in the books.'

The Therapist is clearing her throat, but Tara can't stop. She continues in a tone that's almost apologetic, 'I can tell he feels the same way about me. Every time he goes back to normal, he's genuinely sorry. Every time the rage subsides, he cries for hours. He tells me he hates himself for doing this to me, and I know he means it. He's called me a hundred times already since it happened. I haven't answered, of course.'

'But Tara, if he was so out of control, so blinded by rage, what stopped him at the eye? What stopped him from killing you, for example?'

'He didn't want *to kill me. I don't think he even wanted to hurt me to the extent of sending me to the hospital, you know?'*

'What did he want, then? To give you a small bruise, maybe?'

Tara shrugs. 'Maybe.'

'So he has a line he won't cross. A moral centre, so to speak. He only disrespects you enough to, well, slap you or bruise you from time to time.'

'If there's a good enough reason to,' Tara says, but the words don't sound right outside of her head.

'Do you really believe that, too? That there could ever be a good enough reason for him to hurt you?'

She shakes her head, and yet she'd held this belief inside her all these months like her ultimate truth, repeating I probably deserved it *like a mantra.*

'It made me sick, you know, how you defended him to the police. How you made me promise I won't tell uncle and aunty,' Ahana had later told her at the hospital. Her words had felt like another slap in Tara's face.

'There is no Dr Jekyll or Mr Hyde, Tara,' The Therapist tells her. 'He is always in control. He knows exactly what he's doing to you. He just led you to believe he doesn't. And now you're trapped in a cycle with him. A cycle where he acts like he is your soulmate, and is loving, attentive and kind, to keep you in the relationship. Even then, he's making a mental checklist of all the ways in which you disappoint him. He's still waiting to unleash that other side of him, and you know that.'

Tara squirms uncomfortably.

The Therapist continues, 'I guess you know that better than me, Tara. You even anticipated it, sometimes, didn't you? Looked for signs of when he was going to explode next? It must be exhausting, waiting for which word or what look will set him off. In fact, it started happening sooner rather than later towards the end. Those cycles of euphoria kept getting shorter and shorter. You almost coaxed it out of him to get it over with sometimes, didn't you?'

The Therapist is right, of course. Tara had pushed him that night, too. That's why it felt like it was her fault. She'd baited and berated him to get him to that point.

'No one knows how to push my buttons better than you,' he always told her. Though he was even better at pushing her buttons. He was better at finding her faults and inflating them and making her believe she was worthless, that she'd always be Fatty *and a talentless hack.*

'That part is untrue, and you know it,' The Therapist reminds her now. 'When he met you, he never saw you or expected you to be a person of your own. He wanted you to be an idealized image he had built of you in his head.'

It's nice of her to leave out the part where Tara fed into that idealized image, too. When she worked just as hard at pretending to be whatever he needed Tara to be.

The difference was that when he pushed her buttons too hard, Tara's destruction was neat, inwards and so self-contained – secret binges, too many tears and cigarettes – that he'd barely even hear the 'poof!'

But when she pushed his buttons, he'd make sure she paid.

'How can he love me and still hurt me?' she asks The Therapist, sobbing now.

'Tara, you have to understand he never had any real compassion for you. It was always an act. Men like him, they spend years and years cultivating this cruelty. They have practised the art of distancing from their victims, of depersonalizing them, of turning them into objects in their head. It's ugly, but it's what they need to do to do the things they do to you, and to have that sort of power over you.'

'The good news is that he doesn't have any power over you, Tara. The good news is you don't need to be his victim.'

She could always tell from Adi's eyes when he couldn't see her anymore. The moment she turned from his girlfriend into an object he could kick around.

'It's my anger, babe. I just can't control it.'

That's how Noel had looked at Tara while roughing her up. He had the same it's-nothing-personal expression in his eyes. 'It's just who I am, kitten. A predator who knows no better than his hunger,' she imagines him saying.

She feels something inside her flip. Like someone has pulled a lever that has always been there. Like they lit a match to the bomb she had always heard ticking in her belly. When she explodes, it will be with more than a poof. This time, he'll feel it, too.

She remembers what Ana had seen in her – a honey badger. Relentless, fearless, ferocious. *The prey that bites back.*

'*You're not a victim, Tara,*' she hears The Therapist say now. '*You wrote the very books he is enacting. You know beasts better than he ever will. So why on earth would you not know how to defeat one?*'

Tara recalls all her years spent researching wolves for *Wild Nights with the Werewolf*; how to seduce and tame the predators. But she had learnt how to fight them, too, hadn't she? In the end, hadn't both boiled down to the very same thing?

Step 1: Don't challenge the wolf. Act submissive by bowing down ever so slightly.

The next day, the door unlocks and Noel returns in his morning workout gear of shorts and nothing else, with coffee and croissants and sorrys and another fucking rose.

'It's okay,' she smiles at him. His expression was unsure when he had first arrived – like he was preparing for the morning to go either way, but she sees it soften now. 'I know you didn't mean to hurt me yesterday.

And I know you didn't mean to kill Leo. You're right. He was planning to go to the police.'

Noel reaches out and it takes all her strength not to flinch as his fingers graze the bruises on her neck. 'Does it hurt?'

She gives him another weak smile as she says, 'Only a little.'

'Hold on for a minute,' he replies, returning with an ice pack and a change of clothes for her. His eyes don't leave her as she takes off the bloody night suit and slips into his oversized shirt. The blaze in them gives Tara the courage to whisper seductively and submissively, 'You said you could never hurt me, didn't you?'

He gives her a schoolboy smile. 'Exactly, kitten. That's what I was trying to tell you yesterday, before you made me lose it. Your books spoke to me. That's why the Bodark can't hurt you. You're special, unlike any other woman I've met before. It knows and respects that.'

Step 2: Never, ever run from a wolf or turn your back on one. Don't let it see you as prey.

She bites her lower lip like the women in her books always do. Walking towards Noel, she stops just close enough to look up at him from beneath her lashes. 'Then I want to see you. The real you.'

'Tonight?'

She nods.

His eyes grow dark with desire as he says, 'You sure?'

She nods again, swallowing the urge to scream as she watches his dimples deepen.

When he leaves, Tara waits for the lock and chain to clink behind him, before looking around frantically for an escape. But she can't find any. She surveys each item in the room, inspecting their weight, looking for sharp edges. Even though she doesn't know entirely what to expect, she choreographs a hundred sequences to defeat him in her head. When she's done, she sits down at the edge of the bed, waiting.

He returns hours later, this time as the Bodark. The light of the moon streams in. It feels just like a movie, but a horror one this time. The costume looks so hauntingly real and alive, with crusted blood all over it, white drool dripping from its teeth, it's hard to believe there's a human inside.

The Bodark stands at the centre of the room, snarling, leering. Its yellow eyes fix on her for what seems like an eternity, before it lets out a chilling howl.

Step 3: Remain calm and breathe deeply. Remember, wolves can see, smell and even hear *your fear.*

And so, she sits perfectly still, whispering, 'Is it really you?'

The awe in her voice is real, too. Noel has spent years perfecting this persona. Every part of him seems committed to the act, each one of his mannerisms so akin to a wild creature's. No wonder he had her fooled.

He seems pleased when she says that. He walks towards the bed, his gait unnatural yet natural at the same time. Like an animal walking on hind legs or a human walking on all-fours – or like a creature straddling both worlds.

He's so close now, she can smell the blood and guts on his suit. It makes her choke. He climbs the bed and then sniffs her like a beast would, his movements twitchy.

As the beast's face hovers inches away from hers, Tara feels intense terror unfurl inside her, because she's no longer sure if Noel is still in there. She shouldn't have called him a bad actor because this does not feel like acting at all. She wants to rip off his mask to assure herself there's a human under it all.

Crabs, crabs! She wants to scream now, panicking, but she doubts that the safe word will make him stop. She feels like one of those idiotic people who accidentally fall into zoo enclosures while taking selfies.

Abruptly, she realizes how tiny she is compared to him in his suit. How easily he could rip her apart, limb from limb.

Yet, as he takes her in his arms, her mind once again denies her the highlight reel of her life. All the lit theory lessons she had flunked in college flash through her mind instead, until he is intertwined with Milton's serpent and Rochester's arm. Phallic symbols of destruction. And that one article – about the lion and its trainer.

Step 4: If the wolf comes too close, it's the time to be loud and aggressive. Don't cower away, instead make yourself bigger.

He's too lost in his own fantasy. His grunts and groans disgust her. She is covered in blood and drool.

As he paws at her, Tara feels like she's been freed from some spell. Like she'll never be that woman again. The one who believed she could turn beasts into princes.

She pushes against him, mustering all of her strength. 'I don't want this. Get off! Get the fuck off of me!'

Step 5: No chance of escape? Fight back with everything you have.

At that point, it's kill or be killed.

She screams as she brings the glass lamp down on him. It shatters into a million pieces over the beast's head, some even penetrating its thick fur suit. It looks a bit taken aback, swaying over her unsurely. She uses that momentum to grab a shard of glass to stab it everywhere she can – its back, torso, sides, arms. And then she goes for the neck.

She finds herself unable to stop as she starts to saw at its neck, watching blood and life drain from its body. So driven by the need to be who she isn't – by the need to *prove* it – Tara doesn't stop till she cuts past muscle and tissue and finally, pulverizes the bones. Until its head severs untidily from the neck.

She grabs the head of the man and the beast, and sits back in bed, cradling it.

That's how they find her a day later.

Catatonic and still clutching the dismembered head in her arms, like a trophy.

Epilogue

One year later

The banner, the balloons, the three-tier cake shaped like a wolf – it's all a bit much, Tara feels, as she walks into The Clique in Baga. The seaside pub is packed, with more than half the crowd here to see Tara.

'There's our bestselling authorrr!' Ahana screams, pulling her in for a hug. Tara is still getting used to the limelight after the bizarre case in Goa made national headlines and turned her into a celebrity overnight. When the *The Girl Who Cried Wolf* was finally released, it wasn't just a bestseller, but a huge pop cultural phenomenon, spawning at least two true crime OTT documentaries.

Vik joins them seconds later. 'The woman of the moment! By the way, I have just been discussing the movie rights with these hotshot producers from Bombay,' he motions towards the bar.

Tara scans the crowd and sees Sunny crouched over his phone at a corner table. She wades past the sea of people congratulating her to get to him.

'Congratulations, Miss Tandon,' he grins, as he envelops her in a hug that's way too tight and long, cutting off her blood supply for a good ten seconds. That's how he greets her ever since he led the police to Noel's house that night. He was the one to find her sitting next to Noel's decapitated body, holding his severed head in her hands. The one by her side at the hospital, before Ahana and her parents flew in from Delhi.

'Loved the book,' he says now. 'But I hate how you made me sound like some grumpy cop. I can be fun, too!'

'Sure you can,' Tara rolls her eyes. Lighting a cigarette, she watches a small crowd dance under the warm yellow lights to 'La Bamba'.

For a moment, she is transported back to her first night in Goa. Daria dancing by her side to psychedelic beats, her red hair dazzling against her white gown in the moonlight. That's who Tara has dedicated the book to, along with Noel's other victims and the women of Bliss, most of whom had fled Goa soon after Ana's death. Fortunately, all criminal charges against them were dropped after it was proven that they were acting under duress.

'So, you're the girl ... who cried wolf?'

Tara turns to look at the source of the deep, gravelly

voice. It belongs to a very good looking man in a white linen shirt and charcoal pants. He's nailing the off-duty look, with the sleeves of his white shirt folded up to his forearms, tie loosened and shirt unbuttoned low enough for her to enjoy the bob of his Adam's apple as he talks, as well as the sprinkle of dark hair across his broad chest. He smells like spicy aftershave and his thick hair, though combed back, is unruly. It keeps falling all over the place and into his eyes, and there's something about the way he pushes it back with his hands that makes her stomach flip. Despite the high stools they're sitting on, he towers over both Tara and Sunny. His eyes crinkle and almost disappear when he smiles, a flash of dimples popping up instead. That, along with his broad nose and sharp jaw, makes Tara sigh, as Sunny gives her a pointed *not this again* look.

He is just her type.

'Yeah, yeah, I am,' she replies, smiling ever-so-slightly, even though she knows she is not that girl. Not anymore. She's no longer a prey or a victim, that's for sure. Besides, can't he see her tight black dress? Her perfectly skinny body? She's even gotten rid of those last five kilos, the ones the magazines called the 'most stubborn'. *Look at my fucking straightened and perfectly highlighted hair. Look at how fucking put-together I am! I am drinking vodka and diet coke and eating a salad for fuck's sake!* 'That's quite the book you have there,' he says, and for a moment she warms up to him. 'I mean, I'm not usually into the *Twilight* type of shit,' he clarifies.

Of course, he had to add the disclaimer. They always do when they want to knock you down a peg.

He fixes his eyes – an almost familiar grey – on her as he continues, 'Let me buy you a drink.'

Tara hesitates, wondering if he thinks she's easy prey. She imagines his eyes going panther yellow and his snout twitching as he sniffs her, hoping to find the lingering stench of a girl long-dead. The girl who only lives on in news articles and her latest book.

The new and improved Tara walks around odourless now.

She holds a piece of iceberg lettuce delicately between two fingers, nibbling on it like a tiny rabbit, as he says, 'Come on, I don't bite.'

There's that dimple again. *Ugh.* He's like a plate of fries.

But it's Friday night, there's a whole club of people celebrating her, and Tara finally feels safer than she's ever been. She can have a fry or two, can't she?

'Fine, one drink,' she gives in.

Sunny shakes his head and excuses himself at this point. 'I'll be at the bar,' he whispers in her ear.

The guy scoots closer to her now, his fingers tracing her elbow as he whispers in her ear, 'You're way hotter than I'd imagined. I can't believe someone like you would fall for a guy like that.'

It would almost be a compliment, if it weren't for the subtext. *Were you too idiotic to have seen the red flags, or was it the low self-esteem?*

Tara has faced her share of snark and memes, of course (*'so cringe how she kept falling for that serial killer's shit!'*), but maybe it was all worth it in the end. Now that she was a writer who had come of age, with the novel serving as a classic bildungsroman, as the Goodreads reviews put it. Just like her, they cloaked what happened behind pretentious, artistic terms; the beast reduced to a metaphor and allegory in the end. The online SJWs had even invited her into their fold, now that she'd atoned for her sins, praising her for 'this very important book that would topple the dominant trend of glorification of alpha heroes in modern heterosexual romances, ultimately helping a lot of women'.

'Well, I have learnt my lesson now. That's why I'm not going back home with you,' she smiles at the man. Grabbing her drink, she downs it.

The new Tara knows there's only one red flag in the end and it's *her*. She knows better now than to fall for her type.

Turns out you can totally saw off parts of yourself and sever them from your body, she thinks as she walks away.

Look at me! All healed, exorcized, shiny and new! she all but yells into the night.

And I'll do anything to prove it.

Acknowledgements

A ginormous thank you to—

Anish Chandy, my literary agent, without whom my writing would still probably be limited to my Notes app and angsty Tumblr blogs.

Isha Banerji and Shreyoshee Bandyopadhyay, the dream team at Pan Macmillan India, for all their brilliant edits, suggestions and insights that helped breathe so much more life and magic into *Wolfish*. Udyotna Kumar, for her proofread. Pia Alizé Hazarika, for the stunning cover.

Gundi, Mao and Phoolan, who remained curled up by my side all through this long, long process.

Judith McNaught, my favourite romance writer of all time, whose books have brought me ridiculous amounts of joy since I was a teen.

Most of all, Mom and Dad, for being my endless source of pep talks, unsolicited yet much-needed advice and unconditional, overwhelming love.